Long slender **from behind** ... outstretched arm wa .... as hell as she blindly searched for a towel. She stepped from the tub while wrapping the large white towel around her gleaming body. She slowly tucked the ends into the folds that barely covered her moistened, full breasts.

Chad gulped.

Gabriella turned, looked up, and froze.

Chad couldn't have moved if he wanted to. After thinking about her all night, seeing her dripping wet with bubbles sliding down her enticing body had his mind racing. His heart flipped over in his chest. His lower extremities hardened.

His dreams of her did not do her justice, nor did beautiful describe the golden goddess standing before him. The towel did nothing to hide her curves, which were in all the right places. She wrapped the towel tighter around her wet, shower-spattered body, droplets clinging to her moist skin. But it was too late. Her naked body was already etched in his memory forever. He didn't want to apologize, but it was the right thing to do.

She stared at him for a second longer.

"Do you mind?" she whispered, her tone exasperated as water dripped and pooled around her bare feet on the floor.

Chad found it hard to speak.

"Sorry," he finally mumbled backing out the door. "Uh, take your time. Don't hurry. I'll come back later."

"*Damn*." he muttered on his way back to his room. Living with Gabriella Rumsey only a stone's throw from his bedroom was going to be hell.

Nothing Short of a Miracle

by

Carol Henry

Carol A. Henry

Nothing Short of a Miracle

Cover Art by *Kim Mendoza*

The Wild Rose Press, Inc.
PO Box 708
Adams Basin, NY 14410-0708
Visit us at www.thewildrosepress.com

Publishing History
First Champagne Rose Edition, 2013
Digital ISBN 978-1-62830-108-3
Print ISBN 978-1-62830-023-9

Published in the United States of America

Dedication

Nothing Short of a Miracle is dedicated to
my very own Hero—my husband, Gary.

Acknowledgments

To a fantastic editor, Ally Robertson:
thanks for your continued support and friendship.

Chapter One

The local high school chorus' catchy old-fashioned Christmas Carols filled the food court as Gabriella wheeled baby Nina in the small stroller past the grandstand. A backdrop of dark red Poinsettias stacked in layers formed a twelve-foot tall treelike display behind the singing group. Greenery, gold and red ribbons, and large round shiny ornaments were strung everywhere. Scents of cinnamon drifted from the corner bakery. The chorus burst into a new refrain, while a pianist accompanied the cheerful group.

Christmas is coming, the geese are getting fat, please put a penny in the old man's hat. If you haven't got a penny, a halfpenny will do, if you haven't got a halfpenny, God bless you.

Great. She didn't have a single penny to spare to put in anyone's hat, let alone one of the many Salvation Army's red pots stationed at the entrances of the mall and dotting Ithaca's business-lined city streets.

She wheeled Nina out of the mall into the cold winter weather, winding their way in between shoppers coming and going in the packed parking lot. Horns blared. Disgruntled drivers yelled as they waited for parking spots. Shopping carts blocked the way of others trying to fit in around empty spaces. Gabriella dodged Nina's stroller laden with her purchases through the slush around two teenaged girls giggling and texting on their cell phones.

Oh, to be so young and carefree again. Gabriella sighed. Single motherhood hadn't figured into her well thought-out career plans.

Gabriella tucked Nina in the back car seat, then opened the Saturn's trunk and transferred the formula, disposable diapers, and a new pink baby sleeper she'd found on sale. She folded the stroller and stashed it in the trunk. Her fingers were half frozen by the time she finished and got inside her vehicle.

Although they'd only been inside the mall a short time, it was long enough for the car to have cooled down. She inserted the key in the ignition, hoping to get the heater going right away. The engine coughed, sputtered, and quit.

Crap.

She tried again. This time the motor kicked in and the car purred with a slight hiccup. Gabriella tilted her head heavenward and sent up a silent prayer of thanks.

She looked over her shoulder at her niece, now snoozing away as peaceful as you please. "Not your fault, sweetheart. We'll make it somehow, Nina, just bear with me. I'll do the best I can. I promise."

Gabriella took her time backing out of the parking space, wound the car through the mêlée of holiday shoppers, and left the mall behind. Already store windows were crammed full of holiday decorations and gifts—evergreens, ribbons, bows in varying shades of red, maroon, green, gold, and silver. Gold bells dangled everywhere. Gabriella turned down Hanshaw Road where large old homes were bedecked for the season. She made an effort to soak in some of the Christmas spirit surrounding all of Ithaca in order to get her mind off her dilemma. But no matter how hard she tried, it only served to remind her that her sister and brother-in-law had perished in a fatal car crash. Nina, thankfully, had been at the babysitter's. With no other relatives to care for her, Gabriella didn't hesitate to insist she was the best choice to raise her niece. Dealing with the grief of her sister's death was overwhelming enough, but to have an unanticipated baby to care for made things more difficult. And if she didn't get a grip on her situation soon, there would be no sugarplums dancing in hers or Nina's heads this Christmas.

Tears sprang to her eyes, blurring her vision. Gabriella took a deep breath and wiped them aside. She had Nina's welfare to think of now. As a mature graduate student working on her master's degree, funds were low. She had to deal with the legalities, as well as the care and financial support of caring for her precious niece.

And, she had to face Charles. They had been a couple for almost a year, both of them falling into the relationship first as friends, then romantically. Charles Denton was levelheaded—a stickler for details, and determined to prove to himself and his family that he had what it took to be the best business CEO at his family's firm. To help keep him centered on his business degree, his family had purchased an old Victorian home for him to live in while he concentrated on his studies instead of wasting money on rent. Gabriella was impressed with Charles' drive, and the fact that he found time to spend with her, take her to concerts, plays, and escort her to seminars they both found interesting. Certainly he would be able to help her with a small loan until all the financial ramifications of her sister's estate and the adoption papers for Nina could be worked out and finalized.

Gabriella parked in the circular drive in front of Charles' house and stepped from the car. She lifted the carry seat and the sleeping baby from the back, adjusted the seat into a carrier, squared her shoulders, and climbed the few steps to the front door. The old Victorian home was in the Heights and the only one on the block not decorated for the holiday season. Not that she expected a man living alone to decorate, but a welcoming wreath on the front door would have been a nice touch.

A chill ran down her neck and shoulders, which had nothing to do with the cold winter weather. She wasn't looking forward to having this conversation with Charles. Still, she had no one else to turn to. She had no reason to believe he would be anything other than understanding and supportive. After all, it was only a small loan. They were a couple—couples helped each other in times of need. She needed a loan.

Heart heavy, she rang the bell and griped the handle on Nina's car seat. She waited a minute longer before ringing the bell again. Charles answered the door on the second ring. Gabriella took heart at his smiling face, his sparkling eyes.

Yes. A good sign. A very good sign.

"Hi, Charles, I'm glad I caught you home. Do you have a minute?"

He leaned in to kiss her, caught himself, and jerked back as if he'd received an electrical shock.

"I see you brought your new charge with you."

His monotone startled her. His smile disappeared— his compressed lips looked painful. Definitely not the welcome she'd expected.

"Well, you might just as well bring her in out of the cold," he said. "I don't want to be accused of causing her to catch a cold."

Her spirits plummeted at his sour tone. He stepped aside and held the door open. Gabriella didn't know if she should enter, but she had to get Nina in out of the weather.

"Is this a bad time? Should I come back later?"

Charles had seemed preoccupied the last couple of months, not really giving her the cold shoulder, but near enough that she was beginning to wonder if she'd said or done something wrong to make him act so distant.

"No, no. You're here. Come on in." His entire body stiff as a post, he headed through the well-lit foyer down a spacious hallway assuming she'd followed. Charles all but scuffed his feet as he made his way across the plush carpet toward the sitting room. Gabriella slipped out of her ankle-high, fur-lined rubber boots, and padded behind him down the hall in bright red and green holiday socks. If she wasn't in such dire-straights, she'd turn around and leave.

A fire blazed in the marble fireplace on the far wall—warm, cozy. However, not a stocking hung anywhere—not even a single piece of greenery in sight. Had Charles' home always held this cold and uncaring aura? Just like Charles now? Without unbundling Nina, Gabriella settled the carry seat on the floor next to a chair. Nina slept on, unaware of the tension surrounding them.

Charles stared down his long, straight turned-up nose at Nina as if she had a messy diaper. But Nina was lotioned, powdered, and wrapped in clean, scented blankets. Gabriella's heart smiled just thinking about the cute infant who now belonged to her since her sister and brother-in-law's fatal car accident. Or soon would be legally hers once she found the funds to pay for the legal documents to finalize Nina's adoption papers. The warm fuzzy feelings inside gave her the courage she needed to face Charles and his odd behavior. From the way he carried on, however, she wasn't sure there was ever going to be a good time to approach him.

Charles, hands in his perfectly creased black slacks' pockets, strode across the room to the fireplace, where he stopped and stared into the flickering flames. Again, she had the strongest urge to grab Nina and flee. Her feet refused to listen, however, and she stood rooted to the floor. Was she reading too much into Charles' behavior? Perhaps he was just having a bad day? Too much on his mind, preparing for the semester's finals.

Silence filled the room. The wood in the fireplace crackled and flames spit against the screen. Gabriella jumped at the popping sound as it echoed around the enclosed room. She waited for Charles to say something—anything. But he remained silent. She grew tired of being ignored. She sighed. It was past time to leave.

"I'm sorry I bothered you, Charles. I can see something has upset you. I'll come back another time."

"Don't be absurd. Of course you're not bothering me." He faced her. "Why would you assume I wasn't happy to see you?"

Why indeed? Did he not have a clue as to how preoccupied he'd been lately? Today? How cold and uncaring?

"You don't appear very happy to see me. Did I catch you in the middle of something?"

"No. I apologize." He waved his hands in the air toward the couch. "Where are my manners? Here, let me take your coat. Come sit down. Would you like something to drink?"

"Thanks, no."

His invitation stung of formality. Was he always this formal and she hadn't noticed? Her heart sank. She needed his help. It was now or never. She had to swallow her pride—stand her ground.

"I need a favor, Charles. A small loan. Five hundred dollars. I'll pay you back as soon as I get things squared away…"

"Money?" he hissed before she could finish. "You want me to loan you money?"

Gabriella flinched at his frigid tone. She couldn't be more shocked if he'd slapped her. *Oh. My. God. Where had this stranger come from?* He'd never raised his voice at her before. Never. And he'd never shown any signs of having such a horrible temper.

Nina whimpered. Gabriella ran to her side, kneeled down to make sure she was okay. She longed to pick her up, soothe her. Nina's lips made a cute sucking noise, emitted a deep breath and settled contentedly without a whimper. Gabriella couldn't help but smile. She took a few seconds to clear her confused brain before slowly rising and facing Charles again. She looked into cold, dark, emotionless eyes glaring back at her as if she had two heads and had just presented him with a ransom note for a million bucks instead of asking for a measly five hundred dollar loan.

"I'm not asking you to *give* it to me, Charles, just

7

loan it to me. I…"

"I suppose it has something to do with you becoming the mother of a three-month old?" He cut her off, pointing at Nina.

Whoa. Who was this man who stood in front of her with his hands on his hips, his stance defensive? His jaw jutted forward?

Gabriella clamped her mouth tight, not wanting to say something to make matters worse. Was this the man she loved? The one she had hoped to marry and had wanted to father her own children some day? She had to get to the bottom of his extreme behavior and find out what had him in such a frosty mood.

"Charles, what is wrong? Why are you acting this way? Is it Nina that has you so upset?"

"Do I have to spell it out?" he asked, his hands shaking at his sides. "I'm sorry." His voice softened to a whisper. "I can see I must explain. Our relationship does not include children, I thought you knew that. It wasn't easy growing up in a household full of sisters and brothers all vying for our parents' attention. The noise. The chaos. The competition was fierce. I had to prove myself every step of the way and still do. If I can't prove to my father that I've got what it takes, then I've failed. I don't get to be CEO of the company. And, damn it, I've worked too hard to get this far."

Gabriella swallowed, took a deep breath and quietly counted to ten. She had no idea his background had been so traumatic. Sure, she knew he was driven, but hadn't realized why. As for knowing he didn't want children, they hadn't gotten around to discussing it.

Her insides churned.

"Are you telling me you don't want to continue our

relationship as long as I have Nina?"

"I'm sorry. I'm sure you can see my point." His chin jutted out, his eyes pleaded with her to understand.

A slap in the face would have been much more welcome at this point. He was giving her an ultimatum—a deathblow. Pain ran deep. Hurt, humiliated, regret churned inside. Her stomach blanched.

How could one small child make such a big difference in a person?

"You're honestly asking me to choose between this small baby and you?"

He shrugged his shoulders and continued to look into her eyes waiting for an answer.

"It's your choice," he said, his tone even, unemotional.

"You've got to be kidding me. Charles, I have no choice when it comes to Nina. You must understand that. There is no decision to be made."

Was he really asking her to choose? Was the fact that she'd had Nina for almost a month the reason why he'd been so distant lately? She'd been so involved with caring for Nina, worried about how she was going to cope, as well as getting through the semester with term papers and exams. No wonder she'd missed all the signs. If she'd been more aware, she never would have considered asking him for a loan.

"Apparently, your love for me is not strong enough to withstand one small infant. No, Charles. You made the decision for me. I take back the request of a loan. I wouldn't ask you for money now if you were dripping in it. Oh, I forgot. You *are* rolling in it, aren't you? 'Old Bostonian' money isn't it?"

"You're breaking up with me!" he asked in disbelief, his eyebrows rising clear up into his hairline, obviously anticipating a different response.

Gabriella couldn't believe he was affronted. Well, darn it, she didn't need time to think about it. There was no way she would give Nina up to strangers. She'd figure something out.

"Yes, I am," she said.

She didn't wait for a reply. She picked Nina up and headed for the door, slipped into her boots, and made her way to the car not caring whether or not the door shut behind her.

So much for a happily ever after with Charles.

Gabriella turned down Third Street, tears pooling in her eyes. She blinked to clear her vision and slammed on the brakes for a streetlight that had just turned red. The small Saturn jerked to a stop just short of hitting a family crossing the pedestrian walkway. Her head hit the back headrest. Her heart raced. Good Lord, she'd come close to wiping out an entire family. Thankfully the pavement had been cleared and salted and the car had stopped without skidding.

She turned to check on Nina. Thank God her niece was still sound asleep and unaware of the near catastrophe. Shaking, Gabriella gripped the steering wheel and looked out the windshield where the wipers were still swishing back and forth. The family made it across the intersection to safety, ignorant of their near dilemma. Gabriella let out the breath she'd been holding. Instead of those visions of sugarplums, the macabre scene of her sister and brother-in-law's mangled car wrapped around a tree and her sister laying in the hospital bed dying swirled around in her head.

She gulped back the sadness and sent up a prayer that things would work out somehow. Heaven only knew she didn't need anything else to go wrong right now. What she needed was nothing short of a miracle.

Crunch!

Gabriella's car jolted forward. Once again her head swung forward then slammed back against the headrest. She held her breath, stunned.

"Isn't anyone up there listening?" *What if I'd been killed like Karen and Tom? Who would take care of Nina? What if Nina had been injured?*

"Dear, Lord. Let Nina be okay."

She wiped at her tears that had a mind of their own as they trailed down her cheeks. Once again she leaned over the back seat to make sure Nina was safe. Her niece's pudgy cheeks were smooth and rosy, her lower lip snug against the top lip fluttered, then settled with a soft sigh. Gabriella took another deep, steadying breath. More tears sprang to her eyes.

Gabriella scanned the intersection. Aside from the vehicle that had just rear-ended her, the street was quiet, empty. Light snowflakes drifted down in lazy swirls. Gabriella turned the motor off, unfastened her seatbelt, and stepped from the car. Her legs buckled. A pair of strong arms caught her before she hit the pavement.

Gabriella looked up to find a pair of dazzling ice-blue eyes glaring down at her. His touch sent a warm jolt up her arm. She looked down to where firm, very strong, well-manicured hands gripped her coat sleeve. She shuddered. She gulped in the cold winter air, let it out slowly, and stepped back against the car for support. She looked up at him—he was standing much too close. His rugged good looks had her body temperature rising despite the cold winter air. She must have hit her head on the steering wheel harder than she realized if she was this affected by a complete stranger.

Oh, my God, did she just hear bells ringing in the distance? Or were they in her head?

She blinked and shook her head. Puffs of wispy snowflakes floated down around them as if they were standing in a snow globe. Gabriella craned her neck back to get a better look at the stranger. And met those dazzling periwinkle blue eyes. A tuft of dark curly hair stuck out from beneath his hunter-green baseball cap. His compressed lips hinted at dimples. Dazed, she felt suspended in time.

"What do you think you're doing slamming on your brakes like that?" he demanded, shaking her out of her disconcerting thoughts.

The enchanting cocoon of the moment dissolved in an instant. His tone reminded her of Charles.

"God, lady, you could have gotten hurt if I hadn't been paying attention."

He let go of her arm and whirled around toward the rear of her car. Her knees gave out. She leaned back against the car for support wishing he was the one holding her steady. What was it with him? One moment he supported her, and the next he practically threw her aside.

Her gloves still on the passenger seat, Gabriella tucked her hands inside her coat pockets. The man slid his tall frame in between their vehicles to assess the damage.

"My, God." he moaned, and clapped his hand to his forehead. "*Look*," he said, pointing to the front fender of his silver Mustang.

Gabriella, her knees cooperating at last, walked to where he stood and checked out the alleged damage to his car. She didn't see a thing.

"*A dent.* Lady, I just paid good money to refurbish this baby and now look what you've done. If you weren't so irresponsible, this never would have happened."

"Me?" she squeaked, her back straight, her eyes wide. "No way. You slammed into me. And there is no dent, so don't you go turning the tables and blame me for your reckless driving."

She swiveled around to check out her own bumper and froze. "Holy crap. Look what you've done to *my* car. I'm the one with a dented back end."

Gabriella approached him and pointed her finger at his chest. Never one to strike another person, the strongest urge to do just that bubbled up inside. She held back, took a deep breath. Then let him have it.

"I have a real baby in the back of my car. The damage to *my baby* could have been a lot worse than that imaginary dent on *your* bucket of tin." Anger surged through her at his offended expression. "You crashed into *me*. Not the other way 'round. I was the responsible one. I obeyed the rules of the road. I stopped for a red light. I am in the right. Not you."

She let out an exasperated sigh and continued to poke her finger at his chest. "You, sir, were following too close, weren't paying attention, and rammed into me. The least you could do is *ask* if I'm hurt or if the baby is okay."

He abruptly turned and opened the back door where Nina was strapped into her car seat.

"Stop!" Gabriella screamed. "What do you think you're doing? Don't you touch my baby. You're a stranger for God's sake. Get back."

Gabriella flew at him, pushed him aside with a strength she didn't know she possessed. He bumped his head on the doorframe. His hat tilted sideways. Good. He deserved having some sense knocked into his head. His stunned expression would be comical if the situation wasn't so serious. She hoped he ended up with a knot the size of Texas on his handsome head.

Gabriella's chest rose and fell to the rapid beat of her heart beneath her coat now flapping in the cold winter wind. What a crappy day. She didn't need any more problems dumped in her lap. And didn't need this man taking liberties when it came to Nina.

She leaned in to check on her niece. And it hit her like a ton of bricks. She'd referred to Nina as *her* baby.

Oh, my God. It's true. Nina is mine, now. Good Lord. I'm a mother.

Gabriella had a sudden urge to lift Nina out of the car and cuddle her up against her chest. *Is this what motherhood feels like? Warm? Protective?* The sensation was totally unfamiliar, yet extraordinarily satisfying—it was like nothing Gabriella had ever before experienced. She was high with happiness. She'd had Nina for several weeks and as much as she'd cared for and loved the infant, this was the first time she'd truly wanted to keep Nina as her own despite any trials she had to go through—for as long as it took.

"Look, lady," he said, interrupting her contemplations, "I just wanted to make sure the baby was okay."

He rubbed his head. She didn't feel a bit sorry for

his pain.

"What kind of a mother do you think I am? Of course I made sure she was okay before I got out of the car. *Now. Move. Away. From. My. Baby.*"

He didn't go far, but it was far enough. Gabriella slipped back in front of him and leaned in to check on Nina-who was now awake, and puckered up ready to cry.

"There, there, sweetie. You're okay now," she whispered in Nina's ear, giving her an affectionate kiss on the cheek. The baby's lower lip trembled then turned into a smile. Gabriella patted her cheek, tucked the blanket up around her neck, then as quiet as possible shut the door to keep out the cold.

A gust of wind blew Gabriella's hair across her face. She brushed it behind her ears, then thrust her cold hands back in her pockets. She shivered, tugged her coat tighter. A glance at the tall, good-looking man found him still rubbing his head.

She skirted around him and his car, careful not to touch his gleaming Mustang for fear he might accuse her of scratching his baby's new paint job. Ignoring him, she slid into the driver's seat and before she could shut the door, strong fingers gripped her wrist preventing her from closing it.

"Here," he placed a handful of bills in her palm. "This should cover any damage or inconvenience you've suffered. No need to get the police or insurance people involved. From the look of your vehicle, I'd say you don't carry collision any longer, anyway."

"What...?" Gabriella stuttered, looking down, her hand now full of twenty dollar bills. Her stomach churned. If she wasn't in such desperate need of money she'd throw it back at him. The nerve of him insinuating her car was a total wreck. Her Saturn was a perfectly good car. When it ran. It hadn't let her down yet.

Should they exchange names, licenses, and insurance information? She did a quick look around the area and sure enough—no witnesses. Darn it. She looked back down at the money in her hand. *Crap. She'd just been bought off.*

The tall stranger walked back to his car.

"Stop. I need your name and license number."

"What for? You plan on calling me for a date?"

Gabriella's jaw dropped. The jerk had the audacity to smile. And wiggle his eyebrows up and down in a sexually suggestive manner. *Sheesh.* The smile alone made his eyes sparkle through the drifting snowflakes. But she wasn't in the mood to be taken in by his easy banter. Or his money.

"A date? Get real."

"You did ask me for my phone number. I assumed you were interested."

When she didn't answer he continued. "Look, there's no need to turn this in to the insurance company. No one was hurt. I've more than compensated you for your minor dent, while I, on the other hand, am going to have to pay more than twice as much to fix my vehicle."

"So you assumed you could simply turn this around and make light of it, and I'd change my mind?"

He got in his car. The Mustang's engine turned over first time out. Go figure. For a split second she contemplated reporting him for hit and run. Gabriella couldn't believe he was about to walk away from her without the exchange of the usual necessary formalities.

"Wait!" she called to him again. "I think we should call the police."

He rolled down the window. "Look, lady, no one was hurt. Next time, try to be a little more careful driving when you have your kid in the car."

"What?" she squawked.

He had the nerve to stick his head out the window and ask "Don't you have one of those 'Baby on Board' signs, or something? You need to look into getting one."

He backed up, drove the car around her, and took off.

Gabriella sat behind the steering wheel of her own car, open-mouthed, while he vanished like magic in a swirling mist. Then it hit her. *Crap.* She'd just missed the opportunity to take down his license number. She tossed the money on the passenger seat and started the car. Thank heaven it turned over the first time. But the traffic light had turned red again.

The nerve of the man! To think I don't carry collision. Gabriella drummed her fingers on the steering wheel. Well, she *didn't* carry insurance for collision, but it was none of his business. She glanced over at the cash scattered on the well-worn passenger seat, sighed, and did a quick calculation.

"What? Two hundred dollars!" She turned to Nina, who was once again sleeping, innocent of their good fortune.

"Thank you, thank you, thank you," she chanted heavenward. "I'll never doubt again."

Maybe this fender bender was the miracle I needed after all.

Chapter Two

"*OMG*. Gabby, I can't believe he asked you to choose?" Gabriella's college roommate, and best friend for the last six years, jumped from the sofa and ran to her side. "The man is a total jerk." Mindy Crandall lowered her voice and looked at the closed door leading to Gabby's bedroom.

"Nina's asleep. I'm sure she didn't hear you," Gabby smiled. She'd only had Nina a few weeks, and they still hadn't gotten used to having an infant in the apartment.

"I know it's strange, but I keep forgetting she's tucked away in your room sleeping most of the time."

"You've been wonderful. So has Trish. I don't know what I'd do without either of you."

"We're happy to help. I wish I could do more, but I'm in debt in student loans up to my eyebrows as it is."

"Working out our schedules to help babysit Nina so I can go to classes has been a tremendous help." Gabby hugged her friend. "Thanks. I mean it from the bottom of my heart."

Mindy's tight squeeze had tears running down Gabby's cheeks. She brushed at them wondering if she was turning into a permanent crying machine.

"You go ahead and cry, girlfriend. It's about time. Losing your sister and brother-in-law in a car crash just before Thanksgiving is shock enough. How you've managed to hold it all together so far is beyond me. And now to have Charles dump you...here, have a tissue." Mindy swiped a couple tissues from the square box hidden in a red and white homemade crocheted Christmas Santa.

Gabby took the offered tissue and dabbed at her swollen eyes and damp cheeks. But the tears kept falling.

"I'm not sure I'm cut out for this. Maybe I should take a leave of absence next semester and get things sorted out."

"You're tired. You've been on an emotional roller coaster for the past few weeks—round the clock feedings, diaper changes, shopping for baby supplies, studying for semester finals. Why, you haven't had time to adjust to all the changes going on in your life. Neither has Charles. I'm sure once he's had time to think about it, he'll change his mind."

"I don't think so. I just broke it off with him."

"*You. You* broke it off?"

Gabby smiled at the surprised disbelief on her friend's too comical face.

The tears stopped. Gabby sniffed, blew her nose, dried her tear-stained face, then took a deep breath. After today's events, she wasn't sure she could hold up under the stress much longer.

A super soccer mom she'd never be.

And she hadn't even gotten started.

Gabriella had worked hard on her degree—she had one more semester to go before completing her master's. Too bad her history major wasn't conducive to the care of one small infant. Maybe she should enroll in a Human Development class to get some much needed pointers on child rearing.

Her career had been her priority for so long it was hard to think about switching gears now. Caring for a baby full-time was making her life more chaotic. Her once orderly life had been thrown off-kilter.

"You can do this. I know you can," Mindy assured her. "You're doing a great job already, and you're going to be a wonderful mom. Heck, you already are. You don't need Charles, or any other man, to prove that."

"You're right, as usual. You amaze me how level-headed you can be sometimes."

"Right. So listen up. The semester is almost over. Another week. It's the holidays. Stores are always looking for extra help this time of year."

"Are you kidding me? The way the economy is right now? And I'll have to pay a babysitter."

"Don't kid yourself. There are tons of shoppers out there. I don't care what the economists say. I've seen them. Let's check the want ads and see if there's a part-time position available. Trish and I can pitch in and work around your schedule to help with Nina until you can get back on your feet and afford a real babysitter."

Gabby hated to admit it, but for a fraction of a second she'd balked at becoming responsible for the care of Nina after the accident. She'd been in shock. But it only took seconds to admit there was no way she'd turn her niece away. How could she? She was the only family Nina had left. But she hadn't anticipated having to deal with all the legalities. Formalities, really. Tom and Karen's life insurance was barely enough to cover their bills, including medical bills for Nina's birth, and the bank quickly stepped in and assumed the home due to the steep mortgage lien against it. Tom's father was deceased and his mother in a nursing home—he had no siblings. Her own mother and father had died in a plane crash while on vacation five years ago, so she was Nina's only surviving family.

"I didn't think it would be this difficult." She'd already planned to continue her studies and work on getting her career back on track once the adoption was legal and her financial situation became stable. But she had counted on Charles to help get her through. Once they married and settled in to married life, each of them getting their career off the ground, she had assumed they would be able to afford a live-in nanny to care for Nina.

So much for planning ahead.

So much for counting on Charles.

"It seems like all I've done today is cry."

"You're still grieving. It takes time to heal. Add the responsibility of taking care of an infant at a crucial time in your career, of course you're going to think things aren't going to get better."

Gabriella gulped as sadness welled up inside again. Mindy was right. She hadn't had time to deal with the grief of losing her sister.

"A job might bring in enough money to cover a retainer on the legal fees. Once my stipend kicks in next semester, I'll be in a much better position to deal with everything."

"There you go—you have things under control already. Come on." Mindy lifted Gabby up from the sofa by the hand and dragged her into the small kitchenette. "Let's have some hot cocoa and see what the newspaper has to offer in the line of jobs."

Together, she and Mindy spent the afternoon sipping cocoa, scanning the want ads, and making phone calls while Nina slept.

Nothing. All of the holiday clerk positions were filled. *A day late and a dollar short.* An apt expression her father used to say all the time. It fit her current situation. About to start wallowing in despair again, Mindy cried out.

"Hey. Look. I found something." Mindy swirled the newspaper around so Gabby could read it. "There's a couple home-health aide positions listed."

"Home health aides? How am I qualified to be a home health aide? My major is history in case you've forgotten." Gabby looked up in dismay. "What do I know about taking care of the elderly?"

"If you can take care of a three-month old, you can take care of a bed-ridden seventy-year old lady. Just say 'honey' and 'dear' a lot, and accommodate their every need. How hard can it be?"

"I don't know, Mindy, you make it sound too easy. I have a bad feeling in the pit of my stomach about this."

"Posh. There's nothing to it. I once took care of my Aunt Tulane for several months while my mother sailed away on a cruise to 'get away' as she put it. Other than being hard of hearing and having to yell a lot so she could hear me, she basically took care of herself. She was riddled with arthritis and didn't get around much. I made sure she was comfortable, cleaned the house, and did the cooking while she sat in front of the TV in a recliner and dozed most of the time."

"I don't know, Mindy. I hate it when I get those queasy butterflies fluttering around inside me. Like

22

when I visited Charles today. I had this awful premonition before I even knocked on his door, and look what happened."

"You're feeling a bit down. Losing Charles can't be the big loss you're making it out to be, especially knowing how he feels about Nina. Come on, I'll call the agency and set something up for you."

Before Gabriella had a chance to stop her, Mindy had three appointments scheduled for the following Tuesday.

"I'll watch Nina in the morning, but I'm afraid you'll have to take her with you in the afternoon—Trish and I both have labs we can't skip."

Gabby's stomach fluttered.

****

Gabriella checked her watch. *Great.* She was already late. She tapped her fingers on the steering wheel and waited for the heavy traffic to clear. Checking to make sure it was safe, she inched her vehicle out into the left lane and headed toward the Lake District.

The first two interviews had not gone well. What an understatement. The woman at the first interview was bedridden, needed round the clock care, and a medical professional. Gabriella knew without a doubt the woman belonged in a nursing home. The thin, white haired lady hadn't been responsive during the entire interview.

The person at the second interview was so cantankerous, and in the late stages of Alzheimer's. His children's loud, demanding, angry attitude toward him, and what they demanded of a home-health aide, had her shaking her head at the sadness of it all. She definitely wasn't the person for this position either. She hoped the third time was the charm. Literally. She needed a job. However, she wasn't sure it was worth going to the last interview. She had no business applying for a position as a health aide. What was Mindy thinking? Why had she let Mindy make all these arrangements? One of them needed their head examined. Trouble was, she had a feeling it was her.

Gabby had hurried home after the second interview, fed and changed Nina, gulped down a cup of coffee, and bundled them both into her Saturn. She headed out to the afternoon appointment with a Mr. and Mrs. Hempstead. She inched her way through the streets of downtown Ithaca during lunchtime traffic on snow-covered streets, turned up Route 89 on the opposite side of Cayuga Lake. She tapped her fingers on the steering wheel and cursed each red light. She wanted to get this interview over with and chalk the day up to another miserable letdown. She checked her watch while she waited for yet another light to turn green.

She finally found the address listed on the sheet the employment agency provided, and made a right turn onto a long, curving driveway lined with mature, snow covered blue spruce. The grounds surrounding the house reminded her of a Christmas card dotted with red cardinals perched on coated branches and Cinderella-type animals snuggled underneath. In the distance, a gigantic yard lay covered in snow, dotted with bare maple trees, and sloped down toward the water's edge. It was a great yard for children to romp around in, to build snowmen in, or even build an igloo or two. Gabriella remembered the good times growing up in

Pennsylvania and the snowball fights she and her sister used to enjoy with their parents—skating on the pond, searching for the right Christmas tree on their grandparents' family farm.

Despite her melancholy misgivings, her spirits lifted.

Gabriella rounded another clump of trees and stopped in front of an impressive and enchanting three-story Victorian home overlooking Cayuga Lake.

"Just look at this home, Sweetheart." She half turned to Nina. "I bet they've enjoyed some wonderful family holiday gatherings here, too." Gabriella sighed. Tears threatened.

She shook her head and recalled the disappointing exchange with Charles, and the little fender-bender of a few days ago. Had she been too hasty in breaking it off with Charles? The last two interviews were a bust, and already the money the man from the crash had stuffed in her hand had dwindled. What if this interview goes nowhere? Maybe Staffing Solutions could find her something other than a home care position in another week or two.

Right. Who was she kidding? There weren't any other openings at the moment. Other than dog-walking. She had no intention of trudging through the snow-covered winter streets with several dogs yanking and tangling the strings, tripping her and landing in the slush and snow.

Nope. This was her last chance.

Gabriella took a deep, steadying breath, sighed, and got out of the car. She walked around the vehicle and lifted Nina from the back seat. Gabriella smiled at her niece. She had made the right decision—picking

Nina over Charles.

"Well, Nina honey, here goes."

Gabriella kissed the infant on the forehead and tucked the warm blanket over the infant's head. "I'd ask you to cross your fingers and toes, but I know I'd be asking a lot. Just be the cute cuddly baby you are and we'll see what happens." She lifted the sleeping baby from her car seat, and settled her over her shoulder. "Let's get this over with, sweetie," she whispered—her voice wobbled.

Gabriella walked to the front porch, up several steps leading to a set of large double oak doors with enormous fresh scented pine wreaths attached to each panel. She raised the old-fashioned brass doorknocker and let it fall in place. The scent of pine tickled her nose. She took a deep breath, held it, then let it out slowly. She was reminded of the hillsides of Pennsylvania at the family farm and warm memories of the many holidays shared with her sister. She closed her eyes wishing she could experience them again with Nina.

The door opened wide and a rotund, middle-aged woman greeted her along with a great stream of warm, tantalizing holiday spices. The woman's colorful Christmas apron, decorated in tiny gingerbread cutouts along the edges, was dusted with flour. It was obvious she'd been in the middle of baking.

"Hello, I'm Gabriella Rumsey. I'm here to interview for the health aide position with Mr. and Mrs. Hempstead," Gabriella spoke in a rush. "I'm sorry I'm so late."

"That's okay, Dearie, the Hempsteads are expecting you. I'm Ethel, by the way." The woman welcomed her with a lilting voice and a ready smile. "Come on in here out of the cold."

The entranceway was decorated for the holiday season with a wide ribbon of green velvet intertwined along the curved banister of the formal stairway—it took Gabriella's breath away. Boughs of evergreens hung at measured intervals. The foyer, carpeted in an intricate wild dusty rose pattern, ran the length of the stairway leading to the second floor.

"Here, let me take your wee bundle while you get out of your coat." Ethel lifted Nina out of Gabriella's arms with tender care, and drew the blanket back. "Oh, what a sweet babe," the woman crooned.

Nina opened her eyes and let out a wail.

Great. What a way to start an interview. The job was as good as gone.

"I'm sorry. She doesn't like strangers much," Gabriella said, reaching for the infant.

Ethel started bouncing Nina in a gentle, swaying motion, side to side. To Gabriella's amazement, Nina stopped crying. And gurgled and cooed up at the smiling woman for all she was worth.

"Why, she's just a bit tired from being all bundled up in this weather." Ethel held Nina tight against her ample chest and patted and rubbed her back at the same time. "Follow me, now. Mrs. Hempstead is in the library. It's her favorite spot next to the fire. I'll have tea and fresh muffins ready in just a moment. Why don't I keep this wee one with me so you can have a nice chat without being disturbed?"

Gabriella followed like a puppy, relieved for the moment that Nina wasn't fussing.

"You just go on in while I tend to tea," Ethel said.

"They'll be waiting for you."

Gabriella's breath caught when she entered the huge lovely library. A soothing, healing sensation of homecoming enveloped her. Shelves of books lined two of the walls, and a large floor-to-ceiling picture window trimmed in solid oak filled another. But it was the enormous stone fireplace that dominated the room with its bright, cheery fire crackling in the open grate. Gabriella had a quick flashback of pilgrims standing next to a big kettle of soup with bread baking on the hearth.

She didn't see the couple sitting to the side of the room until the gentleman spoke.

"The fireplace has the same effect on everyone the first time they see it." The tall gentleman stood and stretched out his hand. Gabriella's hand disappeared in his large, sturdy, yet gentle clasp. Without a doubt, Mr. Hempstead was king of his castle and dominated the room with his presence. But in a nice way. He smiled, making her feel welcome. The agency had informed her he'd recently had gall bladder surgery—he didn't look as if he'd undergone anything more serious than the removal of an ingrown nail. His warmth and ready smile put her at ease.

"It's breathtaking," she said, referring to the fireplace. "I've never seen anything quite like it."

"No need to apologize, my dear. As I said, we get the same reaction from everyone who sees it for the first time. The house was built in the early 1800s, and this was probably the main meeting room, as most kitchens would have been either downstairs or off in another building. We've added the bookshelves and the large window right after we moved in almost twenty-five years ago. It's our favorite room. Come. Take a look out the window. We have a great view of the lake."

Gabriella followed Mr. Hempstead over to the large window and gazed in amazement at the panoramic view of Cayuga Lake. The lake stretched north for miles.

"No wonder you love this room. The view is fabulous."

"You should see the lake when it's lit up on the Fourth of July during the annual Lights Around the Lake event. It's spectacular. Anyway, with Helen stuck in a wheelchair now, this is a splendid room for her to spend the day recuperating. Isn't that right, my dear?" Mr. Hempstead turned toward the fireplace.

A small woman huddled in an oversized wheelchair, a lap rug tucked over her knees, smiled warmly at them. Mrs. Hempstead wheeled her chair out from around one of the high-back chairs. She was dressed in a burgundy sweater, and every single strand of her snow-white hair was styled neatly in place, forming a bob around her delicate, angelic face.

"I'm pleased to meet you. Excuse me if I don't get up," Helen Hempstead said with a warm, welcoming smile.

Gabriella walked toward Mrs. Hempstead as the woman pushed her wheelchair forward to meet Gabriella halfway.

"You must be Gabriella Rumsey. I hope you found the place without too much difficulty."

Gabriella took the hand Mrs. Hempstead offered only to have Mrs. Hempstead clasp her other hand over top of hers, cupping them. Comforting warmth flowed between them, and Gabriella relaxed. She liked this couple very much. They reminded her of her parents.

"Have a seat, my dear," Helen offered. "Come. Sit by the fire. It's such a windy day today as you can see by the whitecaps on the lake. Now then, why don't we get started before Ethel comes in with our tea?"

Gabriella followed Mrs. Hempstead back toward the fireplace and sank into one of the overstuffed chairs. It would be so easy to close her eyes, snuggle into the deep folds of the seat and take a nap. Having a baby in her room made for a few sleepless nights. Instead, she sat up straight on the edge of the chair, and placed her hands in her lap.

"You don't have to worry about me," Mr. Hempstead told her, looking sideways at his wife. "I'm recovered enough to go back to the office on Monday. Been away too long as it is. Just can't take sitting around here while there are things to be done at the office. Now, Helen on the other hand…"

"Chadwick, you know you shouldn't be returning to work so soon," his wife interrupted. "It won't hurt you to take another week off to make sure your health isn't affected. That old stuffy office of yours can wait a little longer."

"I'm fine, dear. You just like having me around the house to wait on you and keep you company." He turned to Gabriella and smiled. "We made up our minds to hire someone to keep Helen company so I can go back to work without a guilty conscience. I'm not good at sitting around all day—even at my age."

"I do have Ethel, dear. But you're right. She is busy enough as it is keeping up with everything now that the holidays are here and our son has come for a visit. I'm usually very active," she said. "But this hip has set me back making more work for everyone else."

Her eyes twinkled, her lips a broad grin defined the fine bone structure of her rosy cheeks. The woman reminded her of Mrs. Claus.

"I do need someone to help out on occasion and of course, to keep me company while Chadwick is at the office. Now, what can you tell us about yourself?"

Gabriella looked back and forth between the two during their obvious loving married-couple banter. She smiled, liking them even more, and wondered if they would terminate the interview once they found out she was a single parent.

Regardless of whether she had a chance at this position or not, Gabriella needed to be honest. She gave them a brief run down on her situation. About to tell them about Nina, Ethel entered the room maneuvering a teacart loaded with a heaping platter of pumpkin muffins and a steaming pot of tea with one hand. In the other, she tugged a small bassinet-type carriage on wheels behind her. Gabriella marveled at her ease at dealing with both at the same time. She caught the strong aroma of ginger, cinnamon, and nutmeg and her taste buds started to water.

Mrs. Hempstead spotted Nina.

"A baby! Oh, my, Chadwick… a tiny baby," she clapped her hands together in front of her chest. "Why, you didn't say you had an infant with you." Mrs. Hempstead scolded and beamed at the same time, all but clapping her hands together. "We just love babies, don't we Chadwick?"

For a moment, Mrs. Hempstead looked to be on the verge of tears; she was so excited—truly overcome with joy.

"Thought you might be ready for your wee one," Ethel said, lifting Nina from the bassinet. "She's been a real good baby, she has."

"Well, you just bring her right on over here to me," Mrs. Hempstead said. "Do you mind if I hold her? I just love to hold sleeping babies. Chadwick, I think this is going to work out just fine. Just fine, indeed."

Mrs. Hempstead didn't wait for Gabriella's permission to hold the once-again sleeping infant. Ethel, with careful but firm movements, placed Nina in Mrs. Hempstead's waiting arms. The petite woman, clearly in her element, cuddled the tiny baby who snuggled in her warm welcoming arms.

"Having a baby in the house again is going to be wonderful," Mrs. Hempstead cooed.

Gabriella wasn't sure what had just happened. Had she just been offered the position?

"I thought we'd never have another baby in the house, dear." She looked at her husband. "You know how Chad feels about marriage."

Mr. Hempstead stood shaking his head at his wife, not saying a thing. His smile, however, showed his amusement. And his love for his wife sparkled in his smiling eyes.

Helen Hempstead's eyes were glued to the sleeping baby in her lap. "This is so wonderful, my dear. You can move in this weekend, can't you?" She turned to Gabriella, her eyes pleading.

Move in? Was Mrs. Hempstead asking her to move in with them? This was way beyond her expectations. She hadn't contemplated a live-in position. Especially having Nina. But it would solve a major problem she hadn't wrestled with yet. Her roommates were going home for winter break. She and Nina could stay with Mr. and Mrs. Hempstead and not be alone during the holidays.

"Now, Helen. Don't get yourself all worked up over this baby. It's only to be a temporary situation. Besides, there's Sheila and Sean's new baby, Devon."

"I know. I know. But they live clear the other side of town, and since I've been in this darn contraption I don't get out and about as much as I'd like." The wheelchair-bound woman turned to Gabriella. "I have several grandchildren, and Sheila and Sean just had a new baby boy, but they don't come over much at the moment so I can get my fill of that sweet baby boy. And my girls don't bring my grandchildren to visit because they're afraid the kids will get underfoot and become a nuisance since I broke my hip. But with you here, I'm sure things will change."

Gabriella didn't know how her being there would change things, but she liked Mrs. Hempstead. And it didn't look as if the job was beyond her capabilities.

Mr. Hempstead rolled his eyes at his wife and continued to shake his head.

"Gabriella, you'll have to excuse my wife. She is besotted with babies, even if they aren't family. As you can see by the pictures scattered around the room, we are a close family."

It was hard not to be affected by the warmth filling this house—this home. Oh, how tempting it would be to take this job during the winter break. Until after the holidays. It would be heaven to have time to rethink her life, and determine what was best for Nina.

Mr. Hempstead led Gabriella over to the mantel

lined with framed photographs surrounded by sprigs of evergreen, and red and gold bows.

"These are our three children when they were babies," he said, a smile in his voice. "And here's one of each of them when they were in kindergarten. Now, here's when they were in high school—that's Sheila, and Jodi and here's Chad."

On the opposite side of the mantel, photos of the children when they were in high school and college were also displayed. But before Mr. Hempstead continued, the library doors flew open.

All heads turned as one to see a tall handsome man with ice-blue eyes, and dark curly hair, standing rigid, hands on hips, with a frown on his face sure to freeze hell over in a heartbeat.

"Chad," Mrs. Hempstead called out.

"Son," Mr. Hempstead said, pleased.

Oh, no! It couldn't be! Gabriella gasped and almost choked on the warm dry air caught in the back of her throat. The man who had rear-ended her car the other day was none other than Chad Hempstead.

What were the odds?

The hands of fate had just dealt her another unlucky blow.

Gabriella wanted to crawl under the chair with Nina and disappear.

Chapter Three

"You!" Chad blustered. "What are you doing here? How did you find me?" The unexpected Norman Rockwell-type family Christmas picture he'd walked in on crumbled around him. *How the hell had she found out where he lived?*

He waited for her reaction. Her shaking hands flew to her chest. Her eyes grew round. *Damn, she was just as beautiful as he remembered.* He hadn't been able to stop thinking about her, but to see her here, with his family as if she belonged, made him wonder what she was up to.

"Don't tell me, you've come to set up a date after all?"

"What? A date? What are you talking about?" she stammered.

"Don't you remember? You certainly can't be after more money. I gave you enough to take care of any damages I may have caused."

"Money?"

"Yes, money. Do you have to repeat everything I say?"

Money. Of course she had to be after more money. With women it was always about money. Well, she wasn't going to get any more of his money.

"Of course not—you've just caught me by surprise."

"I just bet I have. So, how much are you asking?"

"Asking? I'm not after your money. I'm here to see about a job."

"Job? What job?" Chad turned to his mother and father who were both staring at him as if he were an alien come to take over the world.

"Mom? Dad? What is she doing here? What job is she interviewing for?"

"This is your home? These are your parents?"

Chad glanced back at the shocked woman. He almost believed she was stunned at the news. But she didn't fool him. Not for a minute. He'd been taken in by the best and this lady was not going to be the next in line to take him for all he was worth.

"Of course these are my parents. How did you find out?"

"I had no idea this was your home. You refused to give me your name, let alone any insurance or contact information."

"Chadwick Junior," his mother interjected. Ethel took the baby before she wheeled her chair forward, looking from him to this woman. "What is going on here? Why are you harassing this poor girl?"

Chad glanced down at his mother. "I'm sorry, mother. This is between this woman and…"

"Gabriella Rumsey," his mother said.

He glanced at Ethel, who had the infant snuggled over her shoulder and whose smile warned him he should be wary. All he needed now was for these two women to start matchmaking again. Well, it wasn't going to work. They had no idea what this woman was up to.

"Her name is Gabriella Rumsey."

"It's between Mrs. Rumsey and me."

"You're wrong, Son," his father said. He walked over and stood next to his wife. "I don't know what this is all about, but I think you'd better sit down so we can discuss it without upsetting Gabriella any further."

"Wait a minute. What do you mean I've upset her? What about me?"

"Sit down and have a cup of tea and some of Ethel's fresh-from-the-oven pumpkin muffins while they're hot. I'm sure we can get this silly misunderstanding straightened out right away."

"Misunderstanding? Job? Just what has been going on behind my back? You didn't mention anything about posting a job. I've been here several days already and you've kept this from me? Just what is going on?"

"Nothing has been going on behind your back, Son. Now come on over here and sit down like your mother told you," his father said. "Your mother and I talked it over and agreed it would be useful to have someone to keep her company during the day while I'm at the office. You know, someone to help her out once in a while when no one else is around. It's not easy being in a wheelchair."

"Yes, and we've had the nicest chat with Gabriella and have offered her the position."

"Wonderful," his father said. "You've already met Gabriella and her baby, so no introductions are necessary."

"It wasn't an official meeting," Gabriella spoke up.

She sounded guilty as hell.

She sat back down, perched on the edge of the chair as if prepared to make a hasty exit. He found it difficult to take his eyes off her. She appeared to be genuinely shocked to see him. Was it an act? Was she up to no good? She had to be after more money. Just like all the others. Why else would she be here?

"Now my dear, why don't you tell me what this is all about," his mother said.

Chad started to answer when he discovered, to his chagrin, his mother had directed the question to Gabriella.

"We were involved in a little fender-bender the other day. There was no damage, so your son didn't feel it necessary to exchange information."

Her emerald eyes turned a deep jade. He enjoyed watching her fidget when he countered with his own version.

"She slammed on her brakes without warning, and I hit the back end of her car. And before you ask, Father, it was an accident and there was no damage, so it wasn't necessary to exchange information or involve the police."

"I knew there was an easy solution to this little misunderstanding," his mother said, snuggling the sleeping baby closer to her chest. She looked down at the infant, then back up. "You see, Chad? Gabriella had no idea this was your home. She's here to apply for the position we posted. Aren't you, my dear?"

Chad looked at the baby in his mother's arms and scowled. She was too affectionate toward the sleeping bundle, too protective. He got the strangest feeling in the pit of his stomach. Just what was this woman and her baby doing already ensconced in his parents' home? And their affections?

Chad picked up a muffin, took a big bite, swallowed, and turned to the woman sitting in his mother's home as if she belonged. She looked back at him with uncertainty written all over her lovely face. Her glowing cheeks from several days ago were now drawn and pale. She looked weary and ready to bolt. A momentary tug on his heartstrings caused him to take another swig of his tea. The scalding liquid burned all the way down and hit the pit of his stomach with a vengeance. *Damn.* He wiped at the sweat beading on his forehead.

Dean Reynolds wouldn't be caught dead in this situation. Hell, Dean Reynolds wouldn't be sitting around drinking tea and eating muffins like a momma's boy. He was more of a Scotch on the Rocks kind of guy—very suave, very sure of himself, and nothing at all like the fool he had all of a sudden turned into. Why couldn't he be more like his number one best-selling character?

"I'm sure you'd be happy to help with all the arrangements," his mother said.

Chad choked on his muffin. "What?" Just what had he missed? He looked up to find Gabriella Rumsey standing, holding her baby, preparing to leave. Good. The sooner she left, the better.

"Chad? You will help with the arrangements, won't you?" his mother asked, her voice louder than normal, as if he were deaf.

"Arrangements?" He swallowed another chunk of pumpkin muffin and washed it down, this time with a careful sip of tea. "What arrangements?"

He cleared his throat and jumped out of his chair. *Shit!* Hot tea sloshed onto his favorite teal wool sweater and penetrated clear through to the skin. He ignored it, not wanting to appear any bigger of a buffoon than he'd already been.

"What? What arrangements? Are you two settling out of court?" He faced Gabriella, scowled, then turned back to his father. "What did you settle on?"

"Whatever are you talking about?" his father asked, eyebrows raised. "I understood you to say there were no damages?"

"Chad? Why didn't you tell us," his mother tisked. "My dear, Gabriella, I hope you and Nina are okay. If you need anything, you must let us know."

"Honest, Mrs. Hempstead, your son gave me more than enough money the day of the accident," Gabriella assured her.

Chad gave the woman credit for trying to win his parents over. Right down to the slight crack in her voice.

He wasn't buying it.

"I gave her two hundred dollars for a little bit of a dent," Chad chimed in. He ran his hands through his hair. What was it with his parents all of a sudden? Couldn't they see what this woman was up to? "You should see her car. It isn't worth fixing. I'm surprised it's still on the road."

"Junior!" his mother reprimanded with his nickname from his younger years. "The least you can do is act like a gentleman. To make up for your carelessness, you can help her move in this Friday."

"Move in? Friday?" He couldn't make head nor tails of this entire disjoined conversation. Now the woman was moving in? No way in hell was he going to let this woman move into his parents' house. *No way!* And definitely no way in hell was he going to help her move in.

"Move in?" he repeated. "Isn't this a bit sudden? Perhaps she should come daily until you see if she suits, if you feel the need to hire her. Have you checked her references? What do you know about her? Can you trust her? Have you interviewed other applicants?"

"Now, Chad. Shush," his mother chided. "Of course we can trust her. We've had a nice long chat, and your father and I both agree we feel very comfortable with the arrangement. Besides, there are several empty bedrooms upstairs. Gabriella and Nina can have Jodi's old room, it's plenty big enough. It's not like you're going to stay over the entire holidays, now is it? I know how you hate all our holiday parties. Gabriella and Nina will be great company for me, and a big help for Ethel."

"The baby?" Chad had to put an end to this now. "How can she take care of you if she has a baby to take care of? Where the hell is her husband?" Chad ignored the guilt trip his mother was laying on him about the length of his stay. It'd been a few years since he'd made it home for the holidays. What with her and Ethel's matchmaking tendencies, it was much easier to stay away as much as possible.

"Now, Chadwick Michael Hempstead Jr., you're just being rude and I won't have it. Your father and I are not feebleminded. We're good judges of character. And, we've made up our minds."

Chad wasn't sure about the good judges of characters. He'd been set up with a few doozies over the years, one of the main reasons he'd stayed away during the Christmas holiday. There was always a party or two where his mother would invite several single women in hopes something would come of it. But he caught the knowing look in his mother's eyes.

He had just lost the battle.

This woman and her baby better not be one of his mother's 'hopefuls,' otherwise, there was no way he would stick around any longer than it took to drive back to the Big Apple. Having to face his ex-fiancée was looking better than hanging out here during the holidays.

****

Gabriella looked back and forth between mother and son. It was obvious this arrangement was not going to work. She didn't care how much she needed money right now, Chadwick Michael Hempstead Junior was here for the duration, and no way was she going to subject herself to his presence. It was no secret he thought she was after the family jewels. She'd go back to the employment agency and beg for help. She lifted Nina up over her shoulder, gathered her purse, and stood, prepared to leave.

Dog walking was beginning to sound like the job of the century.

"You can have your money back." She dug in her purse with her free hand. "What's left of it, anyway. I had to buy formula and diapers. Now I know where you live, I'll pay back the rest when I get it." She turned to Mr. and Mrs. Hempstead. "I'm sorry, I don't think this position will work out after all."

Gabriella couldn't find the money. She dug deeper into her bag. Her hands shook. Her fingers finally connected with the rolled up wad of twenties. She plucked it out in an unintentional dramatic sweep. Cash flew across the room and scattered to the floor.

Right at Chad's feet.

Gabriella cringed. Heat burned her cheeks. Chad looked down at the money. Silence filled the room. Gabriella blinked, mortified. She turned away from the silent couple staring at the pathetic scene she had just created.

The front door seemed miles away.

"I'm sorry, Mrs. Hempstead," Gabriella said again, shaking her head. "I'll ask the agency to send someone else to interview."

Luck was not smiling down on her today.

She was halfway to the door when Mrs. Hempstead called out.

"Wait." She turned to her husband. "Chadwick. Do something. Don't let her leave. We haven't settled on a time for Chad and Sean to help her move in on Friday."

"I'm sorry, Mrs. Hempstead. I'm afraid my staying here is only going to cause friction between you and your son. You don't need additional frustration in your condition, and especially over the holidays."

And neither did she.

"Now, Gabriella, come on back and sit right down here so we can work this minor snafu out. Don't let my son's present behavior bother you. He really is a very nice boy when you get to know him. He's just been under a lot of stress lately and needs a break. This isn't like him at all."

"*Mother,*" Chad's scolding tones flew right over his mother's head. "Mrs. Rumsey is right. Perhaps you should reconsider."

"Chadwick Hempstead," his mother admonished. "You owe Gabriella an apology. Now, give her back her money."

Chad's jaw tightened, his fists clenched at his

sides. Gabriella's own face would be double shades of pink with chagrin if she weren't already embarrassed by his words and his mother's reprimand.

No way did Gabriella want his apology. "Mrs. Hempstead…"

"My dear. Call me Helen."

"Helen. There's no reason for your son to apologize. I understand." A forced apology from this man would be meaningless.

Gabriella looked up at Mrs. Hempstead's son and studied him. His low opinion of her stung. It wouldn't hurt for him to at least offer an apology, however insincere.

Nina whimpered. Dear Lord. She had a baby to consider. She needed this job. Perhaps she'd been too hasty in turning down Helen's offer. Okay, so she'd let her feelings get in the way. She shouldn't let their testy son's suspicious mind influence her. This job was an ideal opportunity to be close to Nina and still earn some money, not to mention there were no other jobs available right now.

That settled it. She'd take the job. She'd move in. Apology or no apology from "Junior." After all, she wouldn't be working for him. She'd be working for his parents.

"Helen, I've changed my mind," Gabriella spoke before she could change her mind again. "I accept the position. Thank you so much for this opportunity."

Chad's jaw dropped. She didn't care. His eyes pierced hers. She took a moment to savor, with glee and much satisfaction the knowledge that she'd just gotten the better of him.

"My dear, Gabriella," Helen said, practically doing

a Snoopy dance in her wheelchair. "It will be our pleasure to have you and Nina stay with us. Now, don't fret. We'll have you settled in no time at all. Won't we Chadwick?"

Mr. Hempstead beamed. "Junior," on the other hand, looked as if he had no idea how to smile. It was obvious *unhappy* didn't even begin to describe his emotions at this moment. His eyes narrowed. If it was meant to dissuade her, he could stand and glare 'til he was blind. It wasn't going to work.

"Thank you. Friday works for me," she said. "If it fits in with your son's schedule, of course." "Junior" could scowl all he wanted. She'd had enough of being intimidated by Charles—she wasn't going to let this man intimidate her as well. She'd done nothing wrong.

"Friday is perfect," Helen said. "It's all settled. Chad will see you and your adorable baby to your car."

"Thank you, Helen, but I can see myself out. You've both been very kind." She excluded "Junior" in her appreciation and her goodbyes on purpose.

"Nonsense. It will be our pleasure to have you and Nina here," Helen crooned again.

The woman was full of tenderness and caring.

Tears threatened.

****

Chad glared at his mother, hoping she'd get the message. But her hands were pointing toward the rebellious woman holding the baby. His mother gave a stern nod, her eyes telling him in no uncertain terms what was expected. *God. He felt ten years old again.* He hadn't been in the house a full week and already his mother was ordering him around as if he were still a kid.

45

He loved his mother, but there were times…

Following Gabriella Rumsey to the front entrance, Chad grudgingly admitted he might have overreacted a bit. Hell, he'd overreacted a lot. It wasn't like him to jump to conclusions, but seeing her so soon after the accident had shaken him. He hadn't expected to see her ensconced in his parents' home all nice and cozy. Having tea. Her baby on his mother's lap as if it were her own grandchild.

The fire all aglow.

The halls all decked out with holly.

Cinnamon, cloves, ginger and other spices he didn't know scenting the air.

Damn. It had caught him off guard. Okay, so at first he'd been excited to see her. Then he'd gotten angry because she didn't belong there. Or maybe it was because she looked as if she did.

Chad sighed, stepped around Gabriella, and grabbed the doorknob—the touch of the smooth metal, cool. He paused.

"My mother is right," he said, looking into eyes a dark mysterious shade of jade. "I owe you an apology."

She stood silent, the baby resting over her shoulder. She wrapped the blanket protectively over the baby's fuzzy head with smooth tapered fingers and turned to leave.

No wedding ring. Chad's eyebrows rose. Perhaps his parents were right. No wonder she needed a job—a single parent and working her way through college.

He opened the door. "I'll see you at nine o'clock Friday morning."

"You don't have to do this. I can manage by myself."

"If my mother wishes it, it's a done deal. You don't want to cross her." He grinned and wondered what it was about this woman that made him blow hot and cold.

"Make it ten, and I'll be ready. I like your mother too much to disappoint her."

"You might be sorry you admitted as much. Just don't let her hear you say it, or your life won't be your own."

He tucked the bills back in the outside pocket of her purse. She didn't bother to thank him or give any indication she knew he had given the money back. She turned and walked to her car.

Chad rushed on ahead and opened the back door so she could position the baby in the car seat. Neither spoke all the while she buckled Nina in, walked around the car, and slipped behind the wheel.

He stood in the cold, not able to take his eyes off her as she put the car in reverse, turned it around, and drove down the drive. A few fluffy white snowflakes lingered, floating lazily to the ground. His heart lurched. He had a strong premonition coming home for the holidays was going to cost him more than the broken engagement he'd left back in the city—and the two hundred dollars he'd given Gabriella Rumsey.

Her car had long since disappeared before Chad, still standing outside in the cold, wondered just what it was about this woman that tugged at his heart. She was stunning with her sexy auburn hair cascading around her perfect oval face, and those green eyes—sparkling emeralds so deep he could get lost in them. There was something more, if he could only put his finger on it.

He smiled, thinking about her stomping her feet

and pointing her delectable finger at him when she had given him what-for in the middle of the street the other day. He'd had the strongest urge to take her finger between his teeth, wrap his lips around it, and give her something to think about besides her anger. Yep. Definitely more stunning when she'd shown her temper. But today? Today she reminded him of Tanya. Tanya who was only in love with his money. And thanks to Tanya, he vowed never to get close to another woman again.

Nope. He liked his life just the way it was—uncomplicated.

Chad shook his head, sighed and walked back inside the house. The sooner he climbed inside his laptop and lost himself in edits for his next Dean Reynolds novel, the sooner he'd be able to take his mind off his mother's new nursemaid.

Chapter Four

There was no disguising the wail of a hungry baby. Gabriella rushed to the refrigerator, got one of the already prepared bottles of formula, and put it in a pan of water to warm on the stove. She rushed back to the bedroom, picked up the crying infant, and laid her over her shoulder and rubbed her back.

"Shhh, Sweetheart, milk is on the way," Gabriella cooed, bouncing Nina up and down on her way back to the kitchen.

It hadn't taken Gabriella long to figure out the difference between Nina's whimper, whine, or wail. The baby had her well and truly trained. And she'd learned to make sure things were ready well in advance so she could deal with whatever situation Nina presented as soon as it arose. But she didn't mind in the least. Nina was the cutest fuzzy-headed, brown-eyed baby girl she'd ever seen.

And she was hers.

Gabriella tested the milk on her wrist. Satisfied it wasn't too hot, she padded into the living room, chose one of the comfortable easy chairs and sat down with Nina in her arms for feeding time. Gabriella was surprised at how active and alert her niece had become at three months old. Staring at those beautiful brown eyes staring back at her while Nina's rosy pink lips captured the nipple and sucked to her heart's content warmed her insides. It was hard for Gabriella to imagine what she had done before Nina. True, the initial phone call from the police informing her of her sister's accident had changed her world in a heartbeat. There was grief, but now there was also a joy she wouldn't have dreamed possible given the circumstances.

Once half the milk had disappeared inside the small infant's belly, Gabriella laid her over her shoulder and proceeded to burp the wiggly infant. She took the opportunity to change Nina's diaper before she snuggled the baby back in her arms to finish feeding time. She switched to a rocking chair to settle the baby over her shoulder in hopes that she'd fall asleep more comfortably. Gabriella liked this time best. Nina got her undivided attention. She desperately wanted Nina to know she was loved.

Softly, Gabriella sang her favorite Christmas Carols. First *Away in a Manger*, then *Silent Night*, then *Oh, Come All Ye Faithful*. Nina's eyes drooped during the last refrain.

The door opened and Gabriella looked up to find Mindy standing in the doorway. Nina stretched and started cooing.

So much for naptime.

"You're back early. How'd the job interview go?"

"You aren't going to believe me," Gabriella said. She untangled Nina's tight fist that had knotted her bangs, and gave her an affectionate kiss on the forehead. She relaxed Nina in her lap, then brushed her hair aside.

"Try me," Mindy said. She took Nina's hand. Nina clutched Mindy's hand in a tight fist with her pudgy fingers and held on tight, then proceeded to gurgle and coo. "She's such a darling." Mindy smiled, and raised her eyebrows at Gabriella in question. "Come on. Give. What happened?"

Being in the Hempstead's home this afternoon had brought back melancholy memories reminding Gabriella of her own family. She missed them so much. The love and warmth the Hempsteads shared with her was overwhelming. Tears sprang to her eyes.

"Things are looking up. Sort of," Gabriella said. Mindy wasn't convinced. She continued. "You know about the first two interviews not going so well. And that I wasn't looking forward to the last one. And it didn't help when I arrived rather late because of the darn traffic."

Gabriella wrestled with the baby, who wiggled, now wide awake and ready to play. Bouncing her on her knee wasn't an option so soon after finishing a full bottle, so Gabriella pacified her by letting her try to stand. Which proved to be more wobbly, so she put her over her shoulder again and rubbed her back.

"When I got to the last interview, things were going great. Mr. and Mrs. Hempstead are a wonderful couple. They offered me the job and even invited me to move in with Nina."

"That is so cool, Gabby. Wow."

"Yeah, too good to be true."

"You took the job? Right?"

"I almost didn't. At first I did, but then I turned it down."

"*What?*"

"It was the strangest thing. I was having tea and being offered the job when this man who rammed into the back of my car the other day showed up. Of all people, he just so happened to be the Hempstead's son. Chad, short for Chadwick—he's a junior. And, the cretin accused me of being after more money."

"Wait a minute. Whoa. Back up. What's this about someone ramming into the back of your car? When did this happen? You never mentioned anything about an accident."

"Must have slipped my mind after the break up with Charles."

"So tell me more about this man who bumped into your car."

Gabriella gave Mindy the low-down of the accident.

"The jerk stuffed two hundred dollars in my hand and took off without exchanging insurance information. Apparently, he's home for the holidays—staying with his parents. He accused me of tracking him down to extort more money out of him. Like I said, at first I was going to refuse the job. Actually, I did turn down the job. But Mrs. Hempstead ignored me. And, well, I guess I got a little indignant with their son and refused to let him intimidate me. Especially after what I went through with Charles. I had Nina to think about, so I made up my mind to take advantage of the Hempstead's offer and to heck with their cranky son."

"Good for you. Did you inform him you weren't after his money?"

"Who cares what he thinks. Mr. and Mrs. Hempstead remind me of my parents. They made me feel like I was coming home again."

"Are you sure you can handle this? You've been through so much lately."

Gabriella gave Nina a gentle pat. The baby nestled her head in Gabriella's neck. She lowered her voice. "I need the job and the money is good. It will help me with all the legal paperwork. Besides, from what Mrs. Hempstead said, her son won't be staying past Christmas. I'll only be there a few more weeks afterward. If he wants to think I'm out to milk him for every penny he's got, that's his business."

"You've had quite an afternoon. You go girlfriend!"

"I'll be moving out of the apartment on Friday. As soon as I get Nina settled for the night, I'll pack a few of my things. With you and Trish going home over break, we can sublet as planned, if that still works for you."

"Works for me either way. I'm sure Trish won't mind. She should be back before long. We'll ask her. Are you going to have time to study for your last exam?"

"Yes. The last one is Thursday morning. I have a paper due for another class, which is almost finished. I should be able to work on it later tonight after I put Nina to bed."

"Good thing you don't put things off 'til the last minute."

So was Gabriella. Never one to procrastinate, she was ahead on all her assignments and reports. If she could get through the rest of the week, she would be able to move in with the Hempsteads without much stress on Friday.

"I wish I could be of more help, Gabby. You know my funds are limited, too."

"I know, Min. I appreciate the offer. You're a good

friend and I'm thankful for all the help you and Trish have given me since Nina came into my life. I don't know what I would have done without you both."

"Ah, shucks, Gabby. You're going to make me cry." Mindy wiped her eyes. "Are you sure you want to take this job? It doesn't sound as if this man is going to make things easy."

"Yes. I have a pretty good feeling about it even though it's started on shaky ground."

Yeah. Right. Already she had reservations about the arrangements, but she didn't want Mindy or Trish to worry about her. They'd cancel their visits home and stay to help her out in a heartbeat if they thought she was in need. She couldn't keep them from their families during Christmas.

"Right now, I'll take any miracle I can get, even if they come with minor drawbacks."

"I wish I could stay tonight and help you, but I can't. I only returned to change clothes and head out again. Andy and I have plans for the evening."

"Andy?"

"Don't get excited, there is nothing going on. We both have a big exam Friday morning and need to do some extra research. Don't worry, you'll be the first to know if things change. Trust me, Andy doesn't get his nose out of his books long enough to know I exist, let alone to know I'm interested in him. But I keep hoping." Mindy wiggled her eyebrows and smiled. "There's always hope."

"Yes, well, I hope things work out."

Gabriella truly meant it. Mindy was a wonderful person. If only Andy would wake up and take notice. She didn't want Mindy's relationship with Andy to end up like her relationship with Charles.

"Oh, Gabby. Here you are worried about me and my lack of a love life, when you have enough on your plate already. After what Charles did to you, too. The lout. I still can't believe he was so horrible all because of such a sweet innocent baby. How could anyone not love her? You did the right thing by getting rid of him." Mindy put her hands on her hips and shook her head.

They'd had this conversation before, and Gabriella was still stunned over the breakup. The rejection still hurt, although not as much as she assumed it would. What hurt the most was his attitude toward Nina—it was unforgivable.

"I thought he loved me. Boy was I wrong."

"It's better you found out how he feels about kids now, rather than after you were married."

"You're right. I'm just glad I didn't cave into the pressure of moving in with him when he asked several months ago."

"He's such a loser. He has no idea what he passed up."

With Mindy and Trish gone for the evening and Nina down for the night, Gabriella made a cup of tea and settled in bed with her laptop to finish her term paper. But the idea of living with the Hempsteads over the holiday, and figuring out how to stay out of their son's way, kept her awake most of the night. She recalled Mindy's words—"Are you sure you can handle this?"

Right now she wasn't sure of anything.

****

Dean Reynolds was in the middle of solving the crime of the century while still trying hard to keep his mind and hands off his ladylove. They had arranged a secret tryst for later that night and it was all Dean could do to keep his mind focused on the situation he'd suddenly found himself in. Pistol in hand, Dean had just opened the imposing, squeaking doors of the old Martin Mansion, ready to pull the trigger if he had to, and...

Nothing! Not a damn thing!

Chad's mind shut down. With his recent manuscript, *Devils Die Hard* not going very well, his character Dean might just as well go in with a blank loaded in his gun and no back up. *Hell.* Lucinda was going to be lucky if she ever laid eyes on Dean again. Unlike Chad, who had no choice in the matter, he would be on Gabriella Rumsey's doorstep at ten o'clock Friday morning whether he wanted to be or not—packing her up and moving her in down the hall. Well, hells bells, if nothing else, he could keep an eye on her, see what she was up to. If anything, Gabriella Rumsey was easy on the eyes. He'd notice right off, although once he'd seen she had a baby in tow, he'd put a halt on his feelings.

Chad shut his laptop and let out a long sigh. He'd arranged to meet Dennis at The Landing for a couple of beers, so wouldn't have gotten very far on his novel tonight anyway.

Resigned, he changed his clothes, told his father he was leaving, and drove down to the inlet.

The landing was crowded when Chad rushed though the swinging doors—the noise hit him like a sledgehammer. It'd been a while since he'd been here and it hadn't changed in all the years he and Dennis had been coming. A nostalgic twinge hit in the pit of his stomach. *Damn.* The holidays were definitely getting to him. He was starting to let his emotions get the best of him, and that wouldn't do.

Spotting Dennis at the bar, Chad headed in his direction.

The bar and grill was fashioned around boating, especially sailing, a popular sport up and down Cayuga Lake. Dark mahogany was everywhere, especially the bar itself—smooth from the constant rubbing of elbows and sliding of glasses, and the necessary washing and polishing with tender loving care. The entire establishment was decorated for the holidays.

Dennis stepped down off the tall barstool and shook Chad's hand.

"Folks let you out, did they?" Dennis smiled, just like old times.

"Yes. Mother said to say 'hi.'" Chad drew even with a barstool and simply slipped into it, his height not making it necessary to have to step up.

"So, what now? Why the visit home this year?" Dennis asked.

Chad ordered a beer before answering.

"I needed the break. All work and no play. You know how it is. What about you? When was the last time you took a vacation?"

"I haven't been able to swing it. Your father keeps me busy at the office."

"Maybe you should think about dating again. It's been two years since Patti died. Maybe it's time you moved on with your life."

Dennis sighed. He took a long swallow of beer before setting the glass down on the coaster. "It's not easy. You don't fall out of love just because someone you love dies." Dennis didn't speak for a moment.

"Besides, look at you. It took you a long time to get over Tanya."

"Luckily, I wasn't married to her. And I was the one who broke off the engagement. Although she likes to announce that she was the one who left me hanging. Of course that was after she raked me through the courts to try and clean out my bank account." Chad drew in a steady breath. "Look, man. I'm sorry about Patti, but you have to get out there again. Start dating."

"You think I haven't had a date or two? I've tried." Dennis hunched his shoulders. "What about you? You dating anyone?"

Chad could tell Dennis had just changed the subject by turning the tables. Dennis and Patti had been married five years when she developed a rare form of cancer and within months had died in Dennis' arms. They'd had the kind of love his mother and father shared—a lasting love. Much different than the kind of relationship between him and Tanya.

"No one serious," Chad said. "And I don't have any plans to get serious about anyone any time soon."

"Then you're prepared for the parade of 'hopefuls' to begin?" Dennis stated the obvious. "You're leaving yourself wide open coming home without a girl on your arm."

"I know. But I can handle it." Chad chuckled, glad they were on less serious grounds.

"Good luck. Between your mother and Ethel, I'm damn well not betting on you." Dennis lifted his long-necked bottle and took a long draw. Chad followed suit.

"That reminds me, you know the woman I told you about when I met you at the gas station the other day? The one with the baby whose car I bumped into?"

"The foot-stomping mother?"

They laughed, took another drink, and quietly contemplated their own musings for a moment.

"Yeah, her," Chad confirmed. "Her name is Gabriella Rumsey. Imagine my surprise when I walked into my parents' home and found her sitting there with her baby in my mother's arms like it was just another everyday afternoon." Chad proceeded to tell Dennis about the incident that had unfolded. "She already has them wrapped around her little finger. The baby, too. You know how my mother and Ethel are when it comes to babies. All you have to do is put one in front of them, and they're all over it like melted chocolate!"

"So what's this Rumsey woman got to do with your mother?"

"I think she's out for more money from the accident."

"What makes you say that?"

"Like I said, she was at my parents' house when I got home earlier today. I walked in on them. My folks decided they need a nursemaid for my mother. They hired her. Invited her to move in with the baby. Can you believe it?"

"Uh-oh. You are so in deep doo-doo. I'm thinking cupid is about to be conjured up."

"They can conjure all they want, it ain't gonna happen. There is no way I'm ever going to let a woman get her hands on me or my money again. And if you so much as mention I'm a writer in front of her or any other woman, you're dead meat."

Chad recalled with startling clarity how Gabriella Rumsey had thrown his money at his feet, and had refused the position—at first. Probably just a ploy on her part to throw him off guard. No doubt she was after a bigger pay off.

"You know, Hempstead, you've become very cynical since you got involved with Tanya. Not everyone is out for your money just because Tanya was a moneygrubber."

Chad remembered all too well having been hit up by Tanya's lawyer for a financial settlement to "facilitate their amicable separation." Hell, they'd only been engaged a few months. He'd been shell-shocked. But he'd given in after a fight. He didn't want his Bronson B. Brady pseudonym mucked through the tabloids. Giving in had been worth it if for no other reason than he wouldn't have to spend the rest of his life with Tanya bleeding him dry.

No, sir. Marriage was not on his agenda in the foreseeable future.

Chad rubbed his hand across his eyes and down over his chin. He needed a shave. He needed sleep.

"I don't need the complication. And I definitely don't need a baby hanging around. Man, I don't need to get involved in a family dispute or whatever has this woman being a single mother right now. I'm not even sure she was married. There's no ring on her finger."

"Being pretty presumptuous to think she'd want you to get involved with her, don't you think?"

Chad stared at his friend. Dennis was right. His friend had a way of grounding him when he most needed it. What in the hell was he getting himself so worked up over anyway? So, he had helped someone out of a jam by giving her a few hundred dollars, even though the accident was partly his fault. It didn't mean she needed saving. Or he needed to be the one doing the saving.

Even if she was one of the most beautiful women he'd run into—literally. Chad smiled. Gabriella was beautiful in a woebegone, waifish sort of way. But yet, she was feisty as all get out.

"Sounds to me as if this woman is getting to you," Dennis said. "I'd watch out if I were you. You said she was going to be living with your parents? And you?"

"She's not living *with me*. Besides, I'm immune." Chad raised his bottle for the bartender to see, and held up his other hand requesting two. One for Dennis.

"By the way, I need your assistance. I have to help Ms. Rumsey move in."

Dennis whistled softly, then laughed. "This beer's on me. I wouldn't miss this event for all the beer in Milwaukee. Where? When? And what time?"

Dennis' know-it-all smile was asking to be knocked sideways to Sunday. If they weren't such good friends he just might consider it.

"Ten a.m., and don't be late, smart ass, or our friendship ends at 10:01."

****

When Chad arrived early Friday morning, Gabriella had Nina dressed, fed, sleeping, and her boxes packed, stacked, and waiting.

"This is my brother-in-law, Sean," Chad introduced the tall lanky young man who had just stepped from his truck. "And this is Dennis, a friend of the family. He offered to help."

"Define offered," Dennis said, grinning. He extended his hand out to greet Gabriella. "Glad to meet you."

"It's nice to meet you too. Thanks for offering to

61

help."

Chad ignored them. As he walked toward the apartment complex, he motioned for the others to follow as if he'd been there a hundred times.

"Good morning to you, too," Gabriella mumbled under her breath as he passed her.

"It will be once we get this over with," Chad mumbled.

"What? No coffee this morning?" Dennis asked, close on Chad's heels.

"It'll take more than one cup of coffee to make this right," Chad snarled.

Sean stepped between them and extended his hand to Gabriella in welcome.

"It's a pleasure to meet you. Don't let this old grump bother you none, he tends to be like this when he comes home for a visit. He gets a big dose of 'family' and it doesn't sit well. He won't be here very long, and I suspect he'll be out of the house or stuck in his room working as much as possible once the folks start their holiday parties."

"It's good of you to help Mr. Hempstead. Other than the crib, stroller, and a few other baby gadgets, there isn't much to move. My stuff is all boxed up waiting."

"*Chad*," the surly man spit out between clenched teeth. "*The name is Chad*. Mr. Hempstead happens to be my father." He'd already picked up a box from the front porch and was carrying it back to the truck.

The surprised look on Dennis' face was comical. Sean grinned and shook his head. Chad ignored them and put the box in the back of the truck and returned to collect another one.

"The two of you going to stand there all day or are you going to help? Get a move on. These boxes aren't going to move themselves."

"Don't mind him," Dennis grinned. "He had a late night and hasn't recuperated yet. I think it'll take a gallon of coffee to put him in a good mood this morning."

Gabriella thought he was acting like a spoiled brat. She wasn't surprised his mother had referred to him as Junior once. She'd seen the gritted teeth and the wince he'd tried to hide. The best thing to do was to ignore his attitude. She led the others inside where the rest of the boxes were lined up against the wall.

"That everything? Want to do a double check and make sure we have it all?" Dennis asked. He shut the tailgate on the back of his truck, while Chad tossed the dolly up into the back of Sean's already full truck-bed.

The whole process had gone more smoothly than anticipated. Despite the cold weather, the snow had held off and the winter sun warmed everything as it sparkled off the snow.

"I'm all set. There are a few personal items I'll put in the back of my car, along with Nina. Thanks so much for your help. Dennis, it was nice meeting you. Sean, thanks for your help. I'll see you at the Hempstead's." she said.

Sean got in his truck, waved, and took off down the street.

"No problem," Dennis said. "I noticed there's no ring on your finger. Does this mean the father is not in the picture?"

Gabriella was taken aback by Dennis' forwardness. He was a handsome man with his sandy blond hair and his dimpled cheeks, but she simply wasn't interested. Although she liked him already, she didn't want to encourage him. "No. No father," she said, offering no other information.

"Any chance he'll show up unannounced?"

"No."

"Good. Anytime you need anything—a shoulder to cry on, moving out of the Hempstead's, dinner—just give a call."

Dennis' kindness and his flirtation was a balm to her bruised ego after her breakup with Charles, but she wasn't ready to jump into a relationship anytime soon.

"Thanks. I think I'll be okay." Although, help with the moving out part could prove useful if Chad's temper didn't improve. A man with a pickup truck would come in handy.

"Maybe we could do dinner sometime," he said "How about next week after you get settled?"

Gabriella hesitated. "I don't think so, Dennis. But, thanks."

"Dinner isn't a commitment, you know. Besides it'll give you a chance to get away from Chad for a couple of hours."

"I'll consider it. Right now I have too much going on. Perhaps once things settle down."

"You got it. I'll check back with you in a few days."

He shook her hand as if they had just finished closing a deal, except he hung on to her hand a bit longer than a deal called for.

"What's going on here?" Chad asked. He looked directly into Gabriella's eyes as if she was involved in something underhanded. His mood hadn't improved over the past hour and the sour look on his face spoke volumes.

The man needed to get a life. And she didn't think any amount of coffee was going to help.

"Just shaking on a deal," Dennis said, a lopsided grin covering his face. He looked at Gabriella and winked before turning back to Chad.

"Depends on the deal and who's involved," Chad commented, the scowl on his face deepening.

"Lighten up old buddy," Dennis said. "This has nothing to do with you. It's strictly between this beautiful young lady and me. Back off."

Chad's lips thinned, his back straightened. He opened his mouth to speak, but no words came out. After the way he'd acted at the fender-bender, and the other day at his parents' house, she was surprised and puzzled to see him at a loss for words.

She stepped back wondering just how tight their friendship was, and if Chad was trying to warn Dennis off.

"Right," Chad said. "Right." And with a quick nod of his head, his dark hair tumbling down across his forehead, he turned toward their truck. "We're ready to go. Meet you back at the house to unload."

"Don't mind him," Dennis said. "Never did like it when I cut in on his lady friends or beat him to a better deal. I do it just to rile him up a bit now and then. Doesn't hurt to be humbled once in a while."

"I'm hardly his lady friend."

"I know Chad like a brother. Been friends all our lives. I even rescued his sorry self from the lake when we were kids. He thought the ice was thick enough to hold him and his sled. I had to fish him out of the water before he turned into an ice cube. Anyway, Chad never lets the ladies bother him unless there's a reason, usually because they're getting too close. If you only met a few days ago, and you've gotten under his skin already, I can guarantee something is going on."

"He's the grouchiest man I've ever met. Besides, I'm really not interested. I have too many problems to deal with right now to worry about Chad, or anyone else for that matter."

She didn't want to admit to Dennis the real reason she had gotten under Chad's skin was because he assumed she was after his money.

"Are you trying to tell me to back off, too?"

Gabriella's eyes flew open. "Oh, Dennis. I'm sorry. I didn't mean… that is…. I'm so sorry."

"No, no, calm down. I understand. Story of my life. Listen, don't worry about it. I'll call you for dinner, and we can cry on each other's shoulders."

"Thanks, you're a sweetheart." And she meant it. There was a refreshing kindness about him that was hard to resist.

"And don't you forget it. See you back at the ranch."

Gabriella made her way back inside the apartment to check on Nina and collect the rest of her belongings. A few pictures of her family, a special paperweight given to her by her sister when she was sixteen, and the jewelry box containing a couple of precious family gems handed down on her mother's side of the family. The picture of Charles, she took out of the frame, tore it up, and threw it in the washroom's circular file. She didn't want a reminder of what a fool she'd been to think herself in love with such a cold-hearted jerk.

No sooner had she shut the door of her apartment, than Mindy breezed through it along with another spurt of the fresh winter air.

"Who was that gorgeous man who just left with all your belongings? What an irresistible smile—and he even waved at me." Mindy asked, rolling her eyes. "What a hunk. I think I'm in love." Mindy held her hand over her heart dramatically, and pretended to swoon onto the couch. "Be still my heart."

"What about Andy? Isn't he your 'everything'?"

"Fat chance. I caught him watching Veronica. I mean really giving her the eye. Actually, they were so involved with each other they didn't know I was there. So, I figured I'd cut my losses and leave."

"I'm so sorry. You must really be upset."

"It's not as if he ever knew I existed or that I considered him in a romantic way."

"You should've told him how you feel."

"I don't think it would've made a difference. Men! First Charles and you, now Andy and me. What is it with us?"

Gabriella put her arms around Mindy and hugged her. "We'll be just fine. The way you reacted to Dennis, I can't see you being too broken up over Andy right now."

"You're right. Maybe it was just the image of his brain that intrigued me. It did overwhelm me at times— a big turn on."

"You're going to be just fine."

"What about you? You're going to be okay, too?"

"Yes. Mr. and Mrs. Hempstead are wonderful people. I'll give you a call when I get settled. Right now I have to catch up with the others."

"I'll be expecting a complete run down. I'm really going to miss you. And Nina, of course."

"I'll miss you, too. I'm sorry I can't wait for Trish to get back—tell her I said goodbye."

Gabriella gave Mindy another hug, gathered up Nina and her purse, then left her once secure life as a student behind.

Chapter Five

Fifteen minutes later, Gabriella squared her shoulders, maneuvered her vehicle behind the two trucks, and turned the ignition off. The men had already made short work of unloading her pitiful belongings, which were already stacked on the front porch.

She vowed to stay clear of Chad as much as possible while he was home for the holidays. Since she wasn't part of the family, she didn't expect to be included in all the holiday hoopla. Besides, she'd be too busy taking care of Helen. And Nina.

She discovered, however, that Helen had other plans when she and Ethel met her at the door.

"Welcome, my dear. Come in, come in," Helen said. "Ethel and I will relieve you of that darling girl while you go upstairs to supervise the unpacking and get settled."

"I'm grateful for this opportunity, Mrs. Hempstead, especially this time of year."

"Don't mention it, my dear. We're glad to have you. And remember, call me Helen. Now, hand over that precious bundle."

Once Nina was ensconced in Helen's lap, Ethel maneuvered the wheelchair, and the three of them headed toward the library. Gabriella wondered, not for the first time, whether Helen hired her for her services or because of Nina. Regardless, Helen's welcome had been genuine, and warm.

Gabriella's spirits lifted.

"We'll have tea in half an hour," Ethel called over her shoulder. "That should give you plenty of time to sort things out."

"Don't you worry a bit about this small bundle, Ethel and I will take good care of Nina until you come down." Helen waved her hand over her shoulder, dismissing Gabriella. "Take your time."

Sean and Dennis passed her in the hall and headed up the stairs. Their arms were full of the last of the boxes. There was nothing left for Gabriella to do but follow. Chad was nowhere in sight, for which Gabriella was relieved. With any luck he would keep right on avoiding her.

The bedroom was decorated in various shades of rich lavenders and pinks. A white-canopied queen-sized bed covered in chintz and strewn with plump, matching pillows took up one side of the room. To the left of the window, in the corner, was a small crib that looked as if the family had owned it for years—now freshly made up, ready for Nina. The baby motif of pinks and blues with baby blocks and teddy bears, giraffes, and other cuddly animals coordinated with the crib pads, sheets and blankets. Someone had even put a musical mobile over the crib.

A touch of melancholy washed over her. She sank down on the edge of the bed. Her sister would have adored the setup. Touched by the Hempstead's kindness, Gabriella had a hard time holding back the tears. She pinched her thumb and forefinger over the bridge of her nose and took a deep breath.

"Who was the hot looking babe back at your

apartment?" Dennis asked.

She stood and held the door for him as he carted a heavy box into the room and deposited his load on the floor.

"She a friend of yours?"

So much for Dennis being interested in her.

"My college roommate, Mindy. Sorry, I should have introduced you. Unfortunately, she's finishing up her exams on Monday and leaving town on Tuesday."

"Just my luck."

"You don't have any luck, Den, so shut your trap," Sean groused. "Get your butt moving and help me with this box before I drop it on your toes."

"Yeah, right. You're just jealous you're not single and can't look."

"I can look all I want. I just can't touch."

"Keep that in mind," Chad said, stepping out of one of the closed doors to the left of the landing. "You've got your hands full with your wife. Who just happens to be my sister."

Chad's tone was more lighthearted than Gabriella had witnessed earlier. Maybe his mother was right and he wasn't always so grumpy.

"Thanks for helping," she called to Dennis and Sean as they left the room.

Chad lingered in the doorway.

"I know you don't want me here. Believe me, it wasn't what I wanted either. Sometimes you're forced to do things you don't want to do."

"Right. Fair warning. Don't become too attached to my parents, nor let them become too attached to you. They'll only be hurt when you leave. And one more thing. About Dennis. He's on the rebound so don't get

71

any ideas. He's a good friend. I don't want to see him get hurt again by someone who doesn't care."

So much for his good humor. At least he made it clear where they stood. And even though it was none of his business, the need to be honest about Dennis overwhelmed her.

"I have no intentions where Dennis is concerned. Or any man, for that matter. I have enough problems right now, so don't worry, you're all safe from me."

"Listen, I didn't mean anything…"

"Yes. Yes, you did. Don't worry, I'll keep out of your way while you're here, and I'll put back all the silver when I leave so you won't have to come back and count all the knives and forks."

"*Touché.* Look, I think we're getting off to a bad start. I apologize," he said. "Dennis is right. Coming back home always has this effect on me. It takes several days to unwind. I'm sorry."

"Are you apologizing, or is your mother?"

She was immediately contrite. Her words sounded waspish even to her own ears.

His full, sensuous lips lifted into a hint of a smile. He was an extremely tall, handsome man, and his musky scent, mingled with the fresh outdoors, filled the room. It surrounded Gabriella in a heady warmth—his closeness had her heart beating a fast drum-roll.

"I guess I deserved that," he said, looking deep into her eyes. "Mother's right. I do owe you an apology, even though I would have offered it without her suggesting I do so. As the baby of the family, and not married yet, she likes to think she has to keep me in line. I humor her."

His serious gaze turned warm and sparkly. Was he

actually smiling at her? Her heart fluttered again and she couldn't help but respond and smile back. Maybe he wasn't the scrooge she had suspected him to be. But a niggling feeling deep down inside cautioned her to keep her distance.

Before either of them could continue, Ethel barged through the doorway with a sleeping baby in her arms. Chad's warmth from a moment ago vanished only to be replaced with a scowl. He quickly made his escape. Gabriella heaved a heavy sigh of relief. And frustration. Just when they were breaking ground and calling a truce, it appeared he still had reservations about her. And Nina. Maybe, like Charles, his temperament was because of Nina.

Ethel laid Nina gently on top of the cozy bedding, and covered her with the warm downy blanket. Gabriella joined her next to the crib and together they looked at the sleeping babe.

"She's fed and sleeping like a lamb. What a wonderful little girl you have," Ethel said. There was no hint of having overheard the conversation between her and Chad.

"I hope she won't be any trouble. I'll try to keep her as quiet as possible."

"Babies cry, don't you know? So don't you be worrying. Why, she's such a dear. And once Jodi and Sheila's kids arrive, oh, my, there's no such thing as quiet. We don't mind a bit, though, especially during the holidays when they're all so excited about Santa and presents."

"Thank you, Ethel. I appreciate your kindness."

"No need to thank me. Now run along. Helen is waiting for you in the library. She'll be wondering why

I'm keeping you. I'll bring tea in as soon as the kettle boils."

"I'll just freshen up before I go."

"The bath's to the left of the stairs just down the hall."

Gabriella did a fast wash up in the very old-fashioned washroom. The claw-footed deep oval tub had a draw curtain around it, and the washstand stood on its own on the black and white tiled floor. The towels were fluffy and fragrant, but Gabriella didn't waste much time, not wanting to keep Helen waiting any longer than necessary her first day on the job. She must have taken longer than anticipated because Ethel was just wheeling in the teacart as Gabriella entered the library.

"Ah, Gabriella. Just in time, my dear. Come have a seat," Helen called to her.

"I'm sorry if I kept you waiting."

"Not to worry. Come, I'll let you pour, if you don't mind."

"Not at all. Please, Helen, you'll have to tell me what you expect of me while I'm here. As I said, I've never been a health aide before."

"Now, dear, we'll worry about all the particulars later. Let's enjoy our tea and get to know each other."

Gabriella poured tea into dainty china cups that reminded her of her grandmother's. The herbal aroma steamed, filling the room with an inviting and relaxing hint of mint. Cinnamon buns slathered with icing pooled over onto a crimson Christmas platter. Gabriella served them on matching plates.

"These are one of my favorites," Helen said. She nibbled on her confection for a moment. "Ethel is such a wonder in the kitchen."

Gabriella bit into the warm bun and closed her eyes in wonderment. Ethel's fresh creations were better than her pumpkin muffins, and even they were to die for. These were better than anything she'd ever eaten.

"Being in this wheelchair has put an extra strain on Ethel this holiday. I wanted her to be able to enjoy the festivities as much as everyone else. That's why it was necessary to get someone in to help keep me company."

She understood Helen's need for companionship. With her family gone, the loneliness weighed more heavily this year. Without Mindy and Trish, she would have been completely alone.

"Now, my dear. Why don't you tell me more about your unfortunate predicament." Helen reached across the tray and helped herself to another sticky bun. "I have a feeling there's more to it than you're letting on. Getting it out in the open and off your chest will do wonders for your spirits."

"I don't want to burden you with my problems, Helen, you have enough to worry about as it is. You've been kind enough to give me this position, and truly, it's more than enough."

"Nonsense. We have all the time in the world to chat. We can help each other keep our spirits bright this season."

Helen's concern was so genuine, it only took seconds for Gabriella to open up and tell Helen all about the loss of her family.

"Since my sister and brother-in-law were killed in a car accident, I'm the only family Nina has left," Gabriella said.

Helen was easy to talk to, and Gabriella unloaded

all her frustrations, which did make her feel much better.

"So, this baby isn't yours?"

"No. But I'm in the process of legally adopting her. That's why I need a job. So I can pay the legal fees."

"And this is interrupting your entire life, isn't it? Especially wanting to finish your degree?" Helen sipped from her cup. She replaced the dainty cup in the saucer she held in her other hand.

Gabriella indulged in the pastry as well, enjoying Ethel's baking expertise. She didn't want to mention Charles and how he had given his ultimatum. Although Gabriella was well over him, which said a lot about her feelings—or lack of feelings for him, it still stung. But she confided about having to deal with Social Services and the lawyers. Once all the paperwork was approved, and Nina was legally hers, she'd be able to finish her degree and move on.

"Nina is my main concern right now, and I can't thank you enough for helping me out by giving me the opportunity to have her with me instead of sending her to a babysitter."

"Just think of us as family," Helen said. "We're glad to have you."

Helen placed her cup and saucer back on the teacart. "I've invited the rest of the family for Sunday dinner day after tomorrow. I'd like them all to meet you. In the meantime, I won't need your help the rest of the day. You can concentrate on unpacking. Chadwick will be home soon, so you'll have the evening to yourself as well. Ethel will let us know when dinner will be ready. On Monday the physical therapist will be here and we can set up a routine for the rest of the week. Ethel will show you around the place later, so you can become familiar with things around here. If you'll just wheel me back to my room and help me get in bed, I think I'll take a nap."

Gabriella rose and had just gotten behind the wheelchair when Chad walked in. After their conversation and his sincere apology in her bedroom earlier, Gabriella smiled. But once again his smile didn't reach his eyes. He squinted, drawing his eyebrows together in a scowl.

"Are you settled in already?" he asked.

He made it sound like an accusation.

"Almost. As soon as I wheel your mother to her room I plan to finish."

"I thought I'd join you for tea, but I see I'm too late. Perhaps another time," Chad said, walking further into the room. "I can wheel my mother to her room. I've hardly had a moment to enjoy her company since I got home. We won't keep you from your unpacking."

"It will only take me a minute, and her room is on my way…"

"Nevertheless, I'll do it."

"Now, children, don't fight over me," Helen chuckled.

Gabriella's cheeks warmed. Chad ignored his mother's words, and placed his hands on the wheelchair handles. His fingers brushed against Gabriella's. Tiny shockwaves traveled up her arm. She drew back as if stung. His ice-blue eyes showed similar shock. Gabriella backed away.

"Sorry, Helen, of course your son should be the one to assist you when he's near. Have Ethel call me when you need me. I'll be in my room unpacking."

"I'll show you around the place while my mother naps." Chad surprised her.

"What a lovely idea," Helen said.

Gabriella noted a cheerful note in the woman's voice and tried not to let it bother her. The last thing she wanted was to have Chad show her around the large home. She didn't want to be in his company any longer than necessary.

"I don't want to be any trouble. I can wait for Ethel," Gabriella protested.

"No trouble at all. Give me a few minutes and I'll be right back."

****

Chad stood in the doorway, taking a moment to study the woman who was firmly entrenched in his home. Standing next to the flickering fire, he had to admit she looked angelic—her auburn hair falling around her shoulders, glimmering in the fire's glow, lit up like a halo. Her slim figure, attired in a bulky turtleneck sweater and tight fitting blue jeans, caught his attention. His resolve to put her on the spot about her intentions almost vanished. She'd mentioned something about a lawyer when he'd walked in on her and his mother talking earlier. What the hell was she up to? If she thought she could wheedle more money out of him or his family, she had another thought coming. It wasn't going to happen. Of course he would offer her a settlement like he had Tanya and end this fiasco before it escalated and she took his family for every cent she could get. No way did he want his family's name—or his pen name—dragged through the courts.

Chad cleared his throat. "Ready?" he finally spoke and stepped into the library.

Gabriella took her time stepping away from the hearth.

"You don't have to do this," she said, her hands held tightly in front of her. "I'm sure you have other more interesting things to do besides showing me around."

"It's no bother. I have a few things I think we need to discuss."

"I already told you, I don't want anything from you."

"So you say. But I can see you're in a position that says otherwise."

"What is it going to take to convince you I don't need, or want your money?" she stepped forward, emphasizing her words. "That is what this is all about, isn't it? You think I'm out for more money?"

"We need to settle this dispute between us. I figure a sum of somewhere between three and five thousand will keep you from contacting your lawyer about a lawsuit."

"Lawsuit? What lawsuit? There is no lawsuit. I have no intention of starting one."

Gabriella was staggered by the amount he offered. Not only would it pay the lawyer's fee, it would also enable her to afford a reliable day care so she could finish the spring semester and her degree. But she had to be honest. There was no way she could live with herself if she took his money. She refused to be bought off.

"What? You want more?"

"Now you're questioning my integrity? You're insulting. For the last time, I. Don't. Want. Your. Money."

"But it's obvious you are in need."

"You can keep your charity. I don't need you or any other man bailing me out of a situation they know nothing about."

"I know enough."

"So you say."

Gabriella threw his words back in his face. Perhaps he didn't know everything, but as far as she was concerned, he didn't need to know anything.

"Perhaps we should calm down and discuss this rationally. Have another cup of tea."

"I've had enough, thanks. Forget about the tour—somehow I don't feel in the mood right now."

"We need to continue this conversation. Come, I'll show you the kitchen. I'm sure Ethel has more goodies on hand, and as I've missed morning tea, I'm dying to try some of her delicious gingerbread."

Gabriella hesitated, turned, and headed in the opposite direction. He'd anticipated her intentions and blocked her retreat.

"Running away?"

"From what? You? Hardly. I just have better things to do with my time than to stay and argue when I know you won't listen to anything I have to say. Why waste my time?"

He stepped close. She lifted her head to look up at his raised brows.

"Why don't we start with why you talked to my mother about retaining a lawyer?"

"You were eavesdropping?" she accused.

"Don't change the subject. I merely overhead you talking when I walked into the room. So, why a lawyer?"

"If you must know, I've been working with a lawyer in order to get legal custody of Nina."

"Legal custody? The child isn't legally yours? I assumed a mother has all the rights. Is the father trying to take her away from you?"

"No. Her father died in a car crash recently."

"I'm sorry for your loss. If that's the case, there shouldn't be a problem in gaining custody. Are the father's parents interfering?"

"Her mother, my sister, and my brother-in-law, died in a car crash. Nina is my niece. I'm in the process of adopting her. Satisfied?"

Tears gathered at the back of Gabriella's eyes.

"I'm sorry. The baby can't be very old—when did this happen?"

"Just before Thanksgiving."

"Oh, Lord."

He reached for her—she stepped back. She'd been holding her breath, keeping a sob back along with the tears. She cleared her throat to control her emotions, looked back up at him—the sadness in her eyes his undoing.

"Your sympathy is misplaced and not wanted. And now, if you'll excuse me, I really must go check on *my daughter*."

Chad let her go without a word. What could he say? Not only had he misjudged her intentions, he had unknowingly done the unthinkable. He'd bumped into the back of her car while Nina was in the back seat. Gabriella must have been beside herself with grief so soon after the deadly crash of Nina's parents. The fender-bender was sure to have given her pause. No wonder she had been distracted and protective. He'd been an insensitive ass. She must hate his guts right about now.

Chad skipped tea and set out for a walk. The brisk winter air would go a long way to clear his addled brain. He needed to sort things out before he made a bigger fool of himself than he already had. He wasn't usually so obtuse when it came to other people's feelings. But Tanya had changed all that. Still, there was no excuse sufficient to absolve him from his insensitive actions this time.

He zipped his warm, fleece-lined dark blue jacket and wrapped a scarf around his neck on his way through the kitchen. He grabbed a couple of gingerbread men from the cooling rack and slipped out the side door. The iced gingerbread sported raisins for eyes, nose, and buttons down the front. In frustration, Chad trudged toward the lake and the enclosed gazebo next to the dock. He bit off first one gingerbread head and then the other. He'd come down here to the gazebo many times as a kid growing up. It served as a refuge from his sisters, and a place where many happy family memories were made.

He thought about Gabriella, and his heart picked up a pace or two as his active imagination went crazy wild with the possibilities of what he would like to do to her in the gazebo. He closed his eyes and pictured her the way she had looked standing next to the fireplace. He'd been attracted from the beginning, he had to admit. Romantic seductions entailing a certain ginger-haired lady swirled around his head. He missed a step and stumbled along the pathway leading to the lake.

Coming home for the holidays might not have been such a bad idea after all.

Chapter Six

Chad woke late Sunday morning still not able to get over the fact that Gabriella Rumsey lived right down the hall—in his own home. One night under the same roof with her and she had his hormones going crazy. He hadn't slept a wink all night. True, he'd spent most of the night working on his latest novel, but getting through the next day on only a couple hours sleep was sure to test his nerves.

To make matters worse, his mother had called in the troops for Sunday dinner. The whole kit-and-caboodle—kids and all—would be pouring in within a few short hours. A pre-Christmas dinner, his mother called it—a homecoming event in his honor. Bunk. It was nothing more than an excuse for her to introduce Gabriella and Nina to the rest of the clan.

Aware his mother might be thinking of Gabriella as the next "hopeful" meant he'd have to be prepared for the onslaught. If his mother even got an inkling of his unexpected attraction to her nursemaid, well... he'd cut his visit short and head back to the city.

Although yesterday's talk with Gabriella hadn't gone well, he was still ready to offer her a settlement. How to go about it without making it look like charity was going to be a challenge. Perhaps Dennis might have a few ideas to suggest.

Grabbing a change of clothes, Chad padded

barefoot down the carpeted hall to take a shower. His robe hung open, exposing his naked chest. He opened the door, and the second he stepped inside the bathroom, steam swirled around him. Across the room, a mirage of rich moist skin appeared as if in a dream. Long slender legs, hips, breasts, arms, stepped from behind the shower curtain. Gabby's outstretched arm was as seductive as hell as she blindly searched for, and retrieved, a towel. She didn't see him until she stepped from the tub while wrapping the large white towel around her gleaming body. She slowly tucked the ends into the folds that barely covered her moistened, full breasts.

Chad gulped.

Gabriella turned, looked up, and froze.

Chad couldn't have moved if he wanted to. After thinking about her all night, seeing her undressed and dripping wet with bubbles sliding down her enticing body had his mind racing. His heart flipped over in his chest. His lower extremities hardened.

His dreams of her did not do her justice, nor did beautiful describe the golden goddess standing before him. The towel did nothing to hide her curves, which were in all the right places. She wrapped the towel tighter around her wet, shower-spattered body, droplets clinging to her moist skin. But it was too late. Her naked body was already etched in his memory forever. He didn't want to apologize, but it was the right thing to do.

She stared at him for a second longer.

"Do you mind?" she whispered, her tone exasperated as water dripped and pooled around her bare feet on the floor.

Chad found it hard to speak.

"Sorry," he finally mumbled backing out the door, tripping over the wooden threshold into the hallway. "Uh, take your time. Don't hurry. I'll come back later."

"Damn!" he muttered on his way back to his room. He stubbed his big toe on the carpet's deep pile.

Living with Gabriella Rumsey only a stone's throw from his bedroom was going to be hell. After seeing her naked, it was going to be pure torture. It didn't help that he was always bumping and bruising his body parts when in her presence—first his head, now his big toe. He was going to be a total invalid and needing his mother's wheelchair if he didn't watch out and stay out of the woman's way.

Back in his bedroom, he shut the door, leaned against it, and closed his eyes. A huge mistake. The image of her toweling herself left his mouth dried up and his body tight and ready for action. *Damn.* He needed a distraction. Something, anything to get his mind off the woman he had just seen naked. He sat down at the computer in an effort to immerse himself in his work.

Blank. Zip. Nada. Nothing. Poor Dean was no closer to solving the crime of the century than he had been the day before. At this rate, Dean would never solve the murder and get the girl, and he'd never finish his novel.

Chad gave up. He'd probably be thinking of Gabriella Rumsey the whole time he was in the shower, anyway. Wet. Naked. Oh, Lord, he had to stop thinking about her. But when he stepped out of his room to go downstairs an hour later, there she stood, Nina nestled against her chest. He wanted to run to her and take her in his arms. Instead, he stood paralyzed. Her face turned crimson. Nina turned her head away from Gabriella's shoulder and smiled. A slow drool trickled down Nina's chin. The baby's eyes sparkled and blinked just before she turned her head back into Gabriella's neck. Chad gulped. *Was it possible he was jealous of a baby?* She snuggled the baby closer to her chest. A lump formed in his throat. She cupped Nina's head and cradled it protectively. Transfixed, he couldn't take his eyes off her. He had to turn away to keep from making a fool of himself. He wasn't sure why he was letting this woman affect him so, but it had to stop.

Gabriella kissed Nina's forehead.

Chad's heart rate accelerated into overdrive just thinking about those lips kissing him. All over his body. He opened his mouth. Shut it. Opened it again. He had no idea what to say or do. Words failed him, and he was supposed to be a whiz with words. He turned on his heel and headed for the stairs.

"Wait," Gabriella called, her voice strained.

Chad stopped at the top of the stairs. The front door opened down below, and a ruckus ensued. The rest of the clan had arrived for Sunday dinner.

"Listen," Chad barely got out between clenched teeth, trying to hold his riotous emotions in check. "I'm sorry about, well, you know, the shower thing. I should have knocked."

"I know I locked the door," she said, her eyes lowered. "Obviously, the lock is broken."

"I'll take a look at it. In the meantime, maybe we should set up schedules or something."

"That might be difficult, especially with Nina. Maybe we should just post notes on the door when it's occupied."

"Good idea." Chad was almost disappointed. He liked what he'd seen. *Ah, Hell.* He'd better not let his mother get an inkling of his current thoughts in regards to Gabriella Rumsey. A naked lady, mixed with lots of warm, dreamy, schmaltzy holiday feelings that were driving him crazy. Good old-fashioned teenage hormones kicking up. Apparently, you never outgrew them.

"Come on," he said. "We'd better go down before they send the troops up to look for us."

Chad stepped aside to let Gabriella precede him down the stairs. Jodi, Sheila, and their broods waited down below. Jodi's boys, Jason and Jeffrey rushed toward their uncle, while Sheila's two girls, Sara and Brianna, followed more sedately. Sheila held six-year-old Constance's hand.

"Sheila, Jodi, this is Gabriella Rumsey. I'm sure mother has told you all about her. Gabriella, my sisters and their kids. I have no doubt they'll take great delight in telling you all about themselves."

"Hello," Gabriella said. "I'm pleased to meet you."

"If you ladies will excuse me, I'll go find the men. I take it Sean has baby Devon with him." Chad looked from one sister to the other. "Be gentle," he warned. "I know how the two of you devour babies. Gabriella isn't used to a big family."

His words were ignored as his two sisters struggled to be the first to hold Nina. Shaking his head, he turned and headed for the library, leaving the women to get acquainted. Just before he closed the door, he turned back around, his eyes meeting Gabriella's across the hall. She looked from him back to his sisters and found her eyes misting over. She looked overwhelmed. Lost. And completely out of her element. Her face had "rescue me" written all over it—he was tempted to run back to save her. What would his sisters think if he did? He closed the library door, shutting out the squeals of laughter. Gabriella could take care of herself.

"Ah, Chad, how are you, old buddy? Did you get Gabriella all settled yesterday?" Sean entered the library wearing a smile.

"Like clockwork. Thanks for your help. What about you? I see you're tending Devon already. Bonding with your new baby boy?"

"But of course. Would you like to hold him?"

"Nope. Think I'll pass. God forbid I give my mother any more incentives to keep throwing women my way."

Chad did go over and peek at the small bundle being held snugly in his father's arms. Babies were too fragile looking at that age. He had to admit they frightened the living daylights out of him more than just a little.

Chad's other brother-in-law, Jim, joined them. He clapped his left hand on Chad's shoulder in welcome. "See what you're missing? You're just going to have to give in some time, or your mother will be on your back the rest of your life. Can't believe you haven't met up with someone you want to settle down with before now."

"I've had narrow escapes," he said with a laugh, making a joke of it even though those narrow escapes were nothing to laugh at. He wasn't about to make those mistakes again.

"Bring that lovely boy over here, Sean," Helen

called from across the room. "I've been waiting all morning to see my new grandson."

Helen settled the baby in her arms.

"Chad," his mother said. "You realize we're counting on you to carry on the family name. The girls have produced wonderful grandchildren for us, but you are our only son. By the way," she continued as if they were discussing an everyday event in the household, "I've invited Mr. and Mrs. Newell and their daughter, Jennifer, to have holiday drinks with us this evening. Of course, I expect you to be on hand to help your father entertain everyone, what with me in this wheelchair and all. I'm so glad you're here to help us through this busy time of year. And we've invited Dennis, as well. Now, be a dear and rescue Gabriella from the rest of the family before we go in to dinner."

Chad shook his head and headed for the hallway. What was the use? You just couldn't fight city hall—or his mother. At least by inviting the Newell's and their daughter for holiday drinks, his mother was taking Gabriella off the top of her matchmaking list. Hopefully.

Chad didn't even make it to the door before it burst open and children of every shape and size gushed in from the hallway. Behind them, his sisters and Gabriella, arm in arm, laughing and smiling, entered the library.

His heart thumped so loudly, he was certain the entire room heard it above the boisterous ruckus Jason and Jeffery made when they spied their grandparents. No one except Gabriella looked at him. The look on her face, however, had him worried. She had been laughing, too, and it had changed her entire persona.

She sparkled. If he thought she was beautiful before—
she was absolutely radiant, now. His heart beat faster.

Oh, God. Not a good sign.

If he knew his sisters, and he did know them, he
was doomed. He didn't like the looks on their faces
when they raced past him to greet their mother. Their
smiles more a smirk—their eyes twinkling as if they
had a secret they weren't about to share. They were up
to no good, and he didn't like it one iota. Growing up
he'd learned, to his detriment, just how devious his
sisters could be when it came to matters of the heart.
They took after their mother in that regard.

He might just as well pack up and get out of Dodge
before the bullets started flying.

****

Sunday dinner was a noisy, wonderful family
affair. Gabriella loved it. It had been a long time since
she had enjoyed such closeness. Everyone made her
feel right at home, even Chad.

"When are we getting together to pick out our
Christmas trees?" Sheila asked. "The kids have been
bugging me since Thanksgiving."

"Why don't we plan on next Saturday morning?
We can spend the afternoon decorating. Gabby, you're
welcome to join us," Jodi invited.

The kids all cheered and clapped their hands.

Christmas with her sister and brother-in-law in
Pennsylvania last year had been one of the best in a
long time. They had cut down their own tree and the
three of them had decorated it with hand-strung
popcorn and cranberry garlands. They had enjoyed hot
cocoa with miniature marshmallows while listening to
Elvis Presley croon old-time favorite Christmas Carols.

"Thanks, but I should stay and take care of Nina and Helen."

"Nonsense. Of course you can join them," Helen spoke up. "I think Ethel and I can manage one small baby for a few hours. You go out, my dear and enjoy yourself. That's what Christmas is all about—fun family get-togethers."

Gabriella started to protest again, but Chad's sisters stopped her.

"What a great idea. And since Chad's home this year, he can join us, and get to know his nieces and nephews."

To Gabriella's surprise, Chad didn't object. Instead, he stared at her across the table. Those icy-blue eyes of his were penetrating—disconcerting. Did he think she had somehow instigated an invitation? Flustered, no longer able to maintain eye contact, she looked away only to meet Helen's bright and happy face.

"I'd better stay with Helen..." Gabriella started.

"Chadwick will be here so I won't need your company on Saturday. Your weekends are your own. Go. Enjoy yourself."

Helen's endearing smile made Gabriella feel a fraud. Again she wondered why the Hempsteads had bothered to advertise for a health aide. Clearly one wasn't necessary.

Gabriella looked to Mr. Hempstead for approval. He simply smiled, nodded his head in agreement with his wife, and continued eating his chicken and biscuits.

"Oh, boy," six year old Constance called out over the adults' chatter in an effort to be heard. "Are we going to get our tree with the horse and sleigh like we did last year?"

"Yeah," Brianna said. "That was so cool."

"Wow, I can't wait," Jeffrey said, turning to Gabriella. "We didn't go last year 'cause we were in Boston visiting Grandma and Grandpa Stanton."

"I hope it snows and snows so we can ride in the sleigh," Jason said. "That will be so cool."

"Cool," Jeffrey agreed.

The girls nodded in agreement.

Constance looked serious for a moment before turning to her father, Sean.

"Can I wear my new boots?" she asked.

"And your new leggings if you want," he told her.

"Then I hope it snows, too." She smiled from ear to ear.

"It's settled," Jodi said. "We'll all meet here seeing as neither of us have room in our vehicles with all our car seats. Chad, you can take Gabriella with you." She turned to Chad with a challenging smile.

"Lovely," Helen said.

Chad glared at his sister, then at his mother. They acted as if he wasn't in the room—as if he didn't have a say. Both ignored him. He bit his tongue and hung his head in defeat. He picked up his fork, speared a morsel of something left on his plate and shoved it into his mouth to keep from putting his foot in it. The food tasted like sawdust and stuck in his throat. He downed the rest of the water in his glass wishing it was something stronger.

"Now that we've all agreed, shall we take our coffee in the library where we can get comfortable next to the fire?" Mr. Hempstead said. He stood at the head of the table.

"I'm ready for a nap," Helen looked up at him with a yawn.

Gabriella stood to assist Helen with the wheelchair.

"No, no, my dear. You go take care of Nina then come back down to join everyone in the library. I can manage this. I'll see you all later tonight when the Newell's arrive."

****

Gabriella didn't own many festive outfits, but she finally chose a simple ankle-length, jeweled-neck, navy floral velour dress. She slipped into her black Mary Jane Clogs and a pair of gold loop earrings. She swept her hair back in a stylish French twist, holding it in place with a single turtle-shell comb which blended in with her auburn highlights. She swept her bangs to one side, and squirted styling-spritz above her head to hold everything in place.

Before she left her room, she checked on Nina to make sure the baby was settled for the evening. Gabriella tucked the blanket around Nina's toes, kissed her on the forehead, and made sure the baby monitor next to the crib was working. Helen had insisted on the baby monitor so Gabriella would feel more comfortable leaving Nina alone in her room.

Gabriella shut the light off and softly closed the door. Sheila and Jodi bounded up the stairs and met her in the hall.

"Oh, good. You decided to join us after all," Sheila said. "We were on our way to coax you into joining us if we had to."

"Mother told us all about Nina. How awful," Jodi confided.

"It must be hard for you, being an instant, single

mother."

"I'm still getting used to the idea. But I don't want people to feel sorry for me. I'm actually enjoying it."

Sheila and Jodi looked at each other and Gabriella wondered what they were thinking. She didn't like the smiles they gave each other. But when they turned back to her, their expressions were serious.

"Your secret is safe with us. We won't tell a soul Nina isn't really yours," they said in unison.

"It's no secret. Besides, she'll be legally mine before long, so I don't mind who knows. I already feel as if she's truly mine. And being a single mother just goes along with the territory."

"We're here to help if you need anything. Just say the word."

"Thanks. I appreciate your offer."

"Come on," Jodi said, wrapping her arm through Gabriella's. "Let's go join the others. The Newell's are here and you just *have* to see Jennifer. The fun is about to begin."

"What fun?"

"You'll see. Brother Chad is about to be cornered by another one of mother's 'hopefuls.' She keeps hoping Chad will finally find a woman he'll fall madly in love with and ask her to marry him. That's why we call them her 'hopefuls.'"

The two sisters led her down the stairs and into the library. If possible, the room looked even more festive than earlier in the day. Candles flickered in the window, the pictures on the mantel had been rearranged and taller candles had been lit and were casting a warm glow in between fresh pine boughs. The overhead lights dimmed, and soft holiday music played in the background.

Gabriella spotted the Newells right away. It wasn't hard. They stood out like beacons on a foggy night, especially their daughter, Jennifer.

Jennifer, fit to kill, wore a short, tight, red satin dress that hugged every curve, accentuating all her prominent parts. The matching red stilettos gave her additional height. Long blond hair, with deep blue eyes, and full red lips beckoned the male species like a neon light. Jennifer's sex appeal could revive the dead.

Gabriella had accepted a long time ago that she wasn't tall and sexy, or even beautiful. Still, she found it annoying to watch the reaction of men when they were in the presence of a gorgeous woman like Jennifer.

"Jennifer, this is my son, Chad. Chad, I want you to meet Jennifer. Doesn't she look festive tonight?"

"She certainly does," Chad said. He stepped forward and took her hand.

His eyes lit up. Gabriella did a slow burn, reminding herself that she wasn't interested in Chad, or any other male at the moment. She looked over at Dennis. He had the same interest in his eyes, too.

Men!

Without moving a muscle, Gabriella stood transfixed as the other men in the room were just as taken in by this woman's sex appeal.

She turned to see how Jodi and Sheila were handling the situation. From the looks on their faces, they were irritated.

Jennifer wiggled around the room in her skin-tight, very paper thin dress approaching each of the men in turn. Her handshake was more than a mere touch, it was a lingering grasp. What a vixen! The woman was literally lapping up all the male attention and obviously loving it.

Despite Jennifer being the center of attention, Gabriella caught Chad glancing her way on several occasions. His smile caused butterflies to flutter wildly in her stomach. She felt like a love-sick school girl on a first date. Every time he looked her way, her skin tingled and her face heated like a furnace with the thermostat turned up. Just the thought of him having seen her naked had her insides throbbing in places they shouldn't be. Lord, she hoped he couldn't read her mind.

An hour into the evening, however, both Sheila and Jodi had corralled their husbands away from Jennifer's clutches. Which left Dennis and Chad standing on either side of Jennifer—Gabriella feeling the odd person out. No one noticed, which gave her ample opportunity to observe the scene unfolding in front of her.

Jennifer inched her way toward the opposite side of the room, away from the fireplace with Chad and Dennis keeping in step. Gabriella looked up and spotted the greenery hanging from the alcove toward the side entrance. Ah. Mistletoe. It stuck out like a sore thumb that had been whacked with a hammer. Whoever had placed the mistletoe there must have done so after dinner. The "red-siren" inched her way across the carpeted floor, closer to where Gabriella stood with a drink in her hand.

"Why Chad, you naughty boy. I can't believe you did that to Denny. So much for friends. Did you kiss and make up?" Jennifer's cunning voice grated false and shrill.

Gabriella wasn't sure what they had been talking about. Nevertheless, spellbound, she waited to see what Jennifer's next move would be. She didn't have long to find out. Standing directly under the mistletoe now, Jennifer looked dismayed, her eyes wide, her perfectly painted fingernails lying claim to her ample chest where her heart was supposed to be somewhere buried beneath.

Gabriella wanted to vomit.

"Speaking of kissing, I must say, I didn't notice this beautiful sprig of mistletoe and holly hanging here earlier."

Liar.

Gabriella's stomach lurched. Chad must have seen this coming—he wasn't the sort of man to be blind-sided by this kind of woman.

"Tradition is tradition, after all." Jennifer batted her long thick, mascara-laden lashes at Chad, her voice turning low and sultry.

Chad didn't move, but then, he didn't back off, either. Gabriella watched as Jennifer took matters into her own hands and tugged Chad forward. She slipped her arms around his neck, and held on tight. The vixen drew Chad in for a full frontal assault right in front of everyone—her body snug against his. The woman's very generous, sensual lips were plastered against Chad's. Gabriella's stomach roiled at the display. She held her breath, looked toward Chad's parents and sure enough, Helen had seen the whole thing. The woman looked delighted. There was no other way to describe that animated face and those sparkling eyes. Gabriella hadn't wanted to believe Helen was a meddling matchmaker, but it appeared to be true.

Gabriella turned back to the couple still standing under the mistletoe in a tight lip-lock. They made a striking couple.

Not to be outdone, Dennis elbowed Chad and Jennifer aside in the middle of their kiss, grabbed Gabriella's arm, and dragged her to him.

"My turn," he said, then leaned in for a kiss. Stunned, Gabriella didn't have time to respond before Dennis ended the kiss and led her over to the picture window, away from the others.

"What was that all about?" Gabriella asked.

"Sorry," he said. "I couldn't resist. Seeing Jennifer make a play for Chad, I just got caught up in the moment. Sorry."

Thankfully, the Hempsteads and Chad's sisters were still staring in shock at Chad and Jennifer. They hadn't paid any attention to her and Dennis.

"I wasn't prepared—you surprised me, is all. You do know I'm not interested in anyone right now. Right?"

"You've made it clear. It was just a holiday kiss. Think nothing of it."

"If you'll excuse me, I should go check on Nina."

She crossed the room, startled to find Jennifer blocking her way.

"I understand you're an unwed single mother," Jennifer said before Gabriella could make her escape. "How dreadful to have a baby to have to take care of all on your own."

Jennifer's negative implications were clear. The rude woman reminded her of Charles and his attitude toward Nina.

"I'm a single parent by choice," Gabriella said. "Now if you'll excuse me, I need to check on *Nina*."

"Well, of course." Jennifer's smile was pure bitter syrup. "I'm sure you won't be missed."

Gabriella glanced around the library. All eyes were on them. She was unable to read Chad's expression. His lips were clamped, his brows lowered. Was he angry thinking she was the one to cause such a scene? She decided not to hang around to find out—he could think what he wanted. She fled to the kitchen where Ethel had Nina's bottle warming in a pan of water on the stove.

"Thanks, Ethel. You're wonderful." Gabriella gave the woman a hug. "I'm going to miss you when I leave."

"Just doing my job," Ethel said, her warm smile genuine.

"I don't think your job is to watch over me and make my job easier. I'm not sure why I have a job here at all."

"It'll come to you before long, my dear. Miracles, no matter how big or small, never cease to happen, especially this time of year."

"I could certainly use a miracle this year," Gabriella said.

"All in good time, my dear, all in good time."

"Do you have family of your own?" Gabriella asked.

"Did have." Ethel wiped her hands on her ample, red-nosed reindeer apron. "My husband died ten years ago. My son lives out west and works for one of those highfaluting computer companies. Don't get to see him much. I started working for the Hempsteads a year after

99

Ernie died. It's been my salvation, *my* miracle."

"Why haven't you moved out by your son?"

"Never did like the idea of living in California. Traffic? Earthquakes? No thanks. Besides, my son's lifestyle is too fast for me. I'm happy right where I am. Here, now," Ethel wiped her eyes with the back of her hands, "you take this on up to our wee one before she wakes and becomes unhappy. Helps take the pressure off you to be ready when she starts fussing. Go on, now, and be getting some rest yourself. You look done-in."

"Thanks," Gabriella gave Ethel another hug and this time a kiss on her soft cheek. Ethel was lucky to have found a family like the Hempsteads.

Gabriella wasn't in her room five minutes when Nina woke wanting her evening bottle. A half hour later she was back in her crib fast asleep.

Gabriella, on the other hand, was far from ready for sleep. She sat on the edge of the bed and stared at the snow drifting down outside her window. She shouldn't be worrying about Chad Hempstead, or the cruel words Jennifer had inflicted. She had an exam to study for, a baby to take care of, and a job to do. Who had time to fantasize over a man like Chad? She fell backwards into the soft mattress and closed her eyes. Big mistake. All she could see was Chad's eyes staring back at her. She found herself drawn to him despite his opinion of her. No matter how warm all over she got whenever Chad Hempstead walked into a room. No matter how disarming his smile. No matter how devastatingly handsome. She didn't need or want a man in her life.

Yeah. Right.

Chapter Seven

Gabriella spent the following week working around Helen and Nina's schedule. Tuesday and Thursday, Helen's physical therapist arranged to stop by mid-morning, and Gabriella assisted while Nina slept. After Helen's session, the older woman settled in the hot tub for twenty minutes before she laid down to rest. Nina claimed Gabriella's attention for a couple of hours and Gabriella delighted in playing with her niece who was beginning to laugh, coo, and kick about more and more.

Several times Gabriella caught Chad standing in the library doorway watching them. His expression gave nothing away. She wondered what he was thinking, but then Nina would take her mind off her thoughts about Helen's moody son and back on the bubbly baby and her day would brighten once again.

Thursday morning, after Helen finished her physical therapy and was tucked back in her room for a rest, Chad, once again, stood in the doorway for a few moments before surprising Gabriella and this time, stepping into the room. He sat down in the chair next to where she and Nina were playing on the floor.

"I want to apologize for Jennifer's rudeness the other night," he said. "She was out of line."

"No need to apologize for her." She kept her attention focused on Nina. The baby cooed and smiled up at her. "It doesn't matter what she thinks. But she's right. Nina is my responsibility—I am a single mother."

"But you aren't an unwed mother."

His statement sounded more like a question.

"I'm not married, but I do have a baby. In her eyes I guess I am an unwed mother."

"Not in the true sense of the meaning."

Gabriella wondered where they were going with this conversation—why he was defending her.

"Nevertheless, I could see that it upset you and I wanted to let you know that I don't feel the same way Jennifer does."

"Thank you. It makes it easier to live here until after the holidays."

"I admire you for taking on the responsibility of someone else's child, even if it is family."

Gabriella was stunned. Chad actually admired her?

She was speechless. She swallowed and rubbed her thumbs over Nina's smooth, pudgy hands—the tiny fingers gripped her own fingers. She smiled.

The silence stretched on forever. Gabriella wished he'd leave, his nearness prickling the hairs on her neck.

"Cat got your tongue?" Chad asked.

Was he reading her mind again?

"No. I'm just overwhelmed by you and your family. It's beyond courtesy to include me in your inner circle, especially during the holidays. You have a very loving family, Chad. You're a very lucky man. You should come home more often, your parents miss you."

"Yes. I am lucky. Look, I'm sorry if I made you feel as if you weren't welcome, earlier. I hadn't expected to see you again, especially after I bumped into your car. It was quite a surprise to walk into my parents' home and find you having tea with my mother."

The sincerity of it shone in his eyes. He rested his elbows on his knees and leaned toward her. His breath fanned the stray tendrils hanging loose against her neck. The sensation made her quiver. She was reminded once again of their encounter in the washroom and of him seeing her naked. She inverted her head to hide her emotions. But his next words squelched the heat that had crept up her neck.

"I want to work out a settlement on the damage I did to your car." He raised his hands to stop her protest before she could speak. "I know, I know. You said you don't want my help. But I can see how wrong I was to think the little bit of cash I gave you was sufficient."

Gabriella leaned back on her bended knees, her head snapped up, her eyes narrowed.

"Correct. I don't want your help. And you did give me enough to pay to have the car repaired. You're just feeling sorry for me. Keep your money and your sympathy. I don't need either."

She leaned over and gathered Nina's blankets around her squirming body.

"You do need it. Otherwise why are you here working for my parents instead of planning your next semester? Why are you being so stubborn about this? What's wrong with my money?"

"The fact that you thought I was after it to begin with should be answer enough."

He just didn't get it, did he? Yes, she could use the money, but she wasn't looking for a handout from anyone, least of all him. She'd already turned down his generous offer. How much more was he willing to offer to entice her to take his money? It didn't matter—she wouldn't accept any amount. She wasn't about to become beholden to him.

****

"I was wondering if you're ready for a break," Dennis said. "I have reservations at the Landing for Wednesday night. You'll love it, they have great seafood. "

Gabriella was surprised at the phone call, but shouldn't have been. After the kiss under the mistletoe, he'd promised to call—out of friendship. Nothing more. Still, she'd put it out of her mind. A break from motherhood, even for a few hours sounded lovely.

"You don't have to do this, Dennis. Besides, it's short notice."

"What about your friend Mindy. Think she'll babysit? I can drive you and Nina to her apartment and back."

"You make it too easy," she laughed at his persistence. "I'll give Mindy a call. I think she's still in town. Give me your number and I'll call you back."

With her exam successfully out of the way Wednesday morning, and Mindy more than happy to babysit Nina, Gabriella concentrated on getting ready for dinner with Dennis. Her mind, however, wasn't fully on the evening ahead. Immediately after her exam, she'd called the lawyer to see how things were progressing with the adoption papers. She was told that with the holiday in full swing things were backing up and it might take a bit longer than expected to process the paperwork. On the one hand, she was relieved she didn't need to pay the fees right away, but on the other hand, she was disappointed. She called the Graduate School office and applied for a leave of absence for the spring semester.

Knowing she wasn't going to be fit company, she was prepared to cancel her dinner date with Dennis. However, after thinking it through, she decided to go. She might not have another opportunity to enjoy an evening out anytime soon, and Mindy was looking forward to babysitting Nina.

Gabriella had refused Dennis' offer of a ride to Mindy's and instead arranged to meet him at the restaurant.

"You lucky dog," Mindy met her at the door, taking Nina and planting several kisses on the baby's smooth, chubby cheeks.

"I'm not interested, Mindy. Dennis is nothing more than a friend. Why he feels the need to look out for me is beyond my comprehension. I've told him a number of times, I'm not interested."

"Yeah, yeah. I hear ya, girlfriend. I'm just saying if it were me, I'd be giving that man signals."

"Maybe you should go with him instead. I could always cry off. It's probably what he expects, anyway."

"Kidding. You go and have fun. I can't wait to unbundle this darling girl and enjoy her company—I've missed her."

After dropping Nina off at Mindy's, Gabriella met Dennis at the Waterfront Restaurant where the *maître'd* showed them to a secluded table—too intimate for Gabriella's comfort level. A candle burned dimly in the center. The view overlooked the lake. Gabriella glanced through the window at the icy water where white caps listed about like miniature sailboats lost at sea. Lost and alone—like her.

"So, how was your day?"

Dennis' smile should have warmed her heart, but it didn't. Not wanting to be a sad sack, she put on a brave face and laughed as if she was happy to be having a fun night out.

"I passed my exam," she said.

"But…"

"What do you mean?"

"There's a 'but' in there somewhere. I can hear it in the tone of your voice. What's wrong? Are you having a hard time at the Hempstead's?" he asked.

"No. Oh, heavens. No. I adore Chadwick and Helen. And Ethel is such a dear. I'm so pleased to have such a loving, welcoming place to live while I take stock of my life and get back on my feet. I have a chance to get the mess my life has become straightened out and make Nina legally mine."

She could see she'd shocked him.

"You mean she's not yours?"

"She's not legally mine. Yet." Gabriella said, taking a sip of her wine—a mild blush that went down smoothly and gave her a chance to collect her thoughts.

The waitress approached, took their dinner order and left. Dennis took her hand in his and gave it a gentle squeeze.

"Go on," he said, smiling encouragingly. "What do you mean Nina isn't yours?"

Heaving a heavy sigh, she squeezed his hand back and let go.

"My sister and her husband died in a car crash over Thanksgiving. Nina was at the babysitters. With no other family to care for her, I stepped in and plan to adopt her."

She didn't tell him about Charles. Past history was

better left alone.

"It's been hard dealing with my sister's death on top of missing my entire family during the holidays. It's very comforting being at the Hempstead's."

"It didn't help when Jennifer showed her claws the other night, did it? I'm really sorry for my own actions."

"No it didn't help, but then she probably won't be the last person to think of me as an unwed mother. As long as I know the truth, it doesn't bother me. And there's no need to apologize for her. If she had apologized, I'm sure it wouldn't have been as heartfelt or sincere as yours and Chad's apology."

"Chad? Chad apologized? Does he know about Nina?"

Their meal delivered, Gabriella took a forkful of shrimp scampi, enjoying the lemon-garlic flavor, ignoring his questions. She took a sip of wine, set her glass down, and looked across the table at Dennis.

"It's not a secret. The truth of the matter is she is my child now. Why would he even care?"

"Why indeed. Chad's a good guy, but he's had a couple of disastrous relationships, and suffice-it-to-say, he doesn't trust women. He's discovered most women are only after his money."

"That explains a lot."

"What does that mean?"

"He thinks I'm after his money."

"He does get a little testy when it comes to money."

"Well, I'm not after him or his money so he can rest easy. I have too many other things on my mind than to get involved in a relationship. Or worry whether or not someone thinks I'm after their money."

"Sounds like you've been hurt in the relationship department, too. My shoulders are yours if you need them."

Gabriella didn't want to talk about Charles. Or Chad. Charles didn't deserve talking about. Besides, it was over and done between them. Still, the hurt, although not as deep as it should be, was still a disappointment. Having someone there when you need them only to discover they weren't had struck a blow.

As for Chad? Well, she hadn't figured out what he was all about yet. She wasn't sure if she even wanted to know the real Chadwick Michael Hempstead Jr.

****

The morning after her dinner with Dennis, six-inches of fresh snow blanketed the ground. Gabriella sat next to the fire having tea with Helen after her physical therapy when Chad joined them. He made himself comfortable in a chair next to her, then helped himself to one of Ethel's coffee cake muffins.

"So, how was your date with Dennis last night?" he said, taking a big bite out of the warm muffin.

"It wasn't a date."

He swallowed, sipped from the dainty teacup. His ease at handling such petite china made Gabriella's insides warm.

"Yes, well, with Dennis, it's a big deal."

He placed the cup on the saucer he held in his left hand, then placed his right ankle over his left knee. He looked too comfortable and sexy leaning back in the chair. Gabriella turned away.

"I'm sure he considered it a date. He doesn't go out very often these days. It's been a long time since he's been with a woman."

Gabriella wondered what it was with these two men, warning her to tread lightly where each was concerned. Anyone would think she was a *Matahari*.

"He's a big boy, Chad," Helen jumped into the conversation.

Gabriella had forgotten his mother was in the room.

"I'm sure he can take care of himself. What harm did it do for the two of them to go out to dinner? I'm sure Gabriella needed a night out, isn't that right my dear?"

Gabriella blushed.

"Yes, of course," she said. She turned to find Chad's piercing blue eyes boring into hers. She wasn't about to let this man make her feel guilty about something as innocent as a dinner date with his friend.

"We had a very good time. Dennis is a delight—he's very caring. He told me to say hi to you and Chadwick, by the way."

"He is such a polite boy, it's too bad about Patti…"

Nina interjected with a howl. Chad jumped to his feet, and ran to the baby.

"Is she okay? For God sakes, make sure she isn't choking or something."

Concern etched his face. Gabriella side-stepped him to reach the screaming infant.

"She's fine. She's letting me know it's time for her bottle."

She bent over, lifted Nina from the bassinet, and wrapped the blanket around the now whimpering baby. She patted her gently on the back, soothing her, and made her way to the kitchen to warm a bottle. When she returned, Chad stood, watching her every move. Helen stared at her son in astonished silence. She faced Gabriella, put her teacup down on the side table, a wide smile and sparkling eyes etched on her elated face.

Oh, my God, had she just become one of Helen's "hopefuls" because Chad showed concern for Nina?

"Here then, let me feed that darling girl before you take her upstairs and put her down for a nap."

Gabriella handed the baby over to Helen and returned to her chair. Chad crossed the room and stood next to the window overlooking the lake. Gabriella wondered once again what he was thinking. His reaction to Nina's needs wasn't of someone who was allergic to children—an impression that he'd managed to impart from the beginning.

"By the way, Chad, the Stantons are coming to town the weekend before Christmas and of course, we'll have them over for the evening. And, I've invited the Newell's to join us again, as well. Jennifer and you seemed to hit it off last Sunday. Didn't you think so, Gabriella?"

What was Helen up to? One minute she felt as if she was on Helen's match-making list, but now it was evident Helen was playing matchmaker between her son and Jennifer. She didn't want to get in the middle. Thankfully, she was saved from having to reply.

"*Mother!*" Chad exclaimed, obviously embarrassed.

"Yes, Chad?" Helen looked at her son with such an innocent expression Gabriella wanted to laugh.

"No matchmaking," Chad said, sternly.

Helen paid no attention to his tone. Gabriella smiled—the interaction between mother and son amusing.

"I'm wounded," Helen said. She put Nina over her shoulder and proceeded to burp the now content baby. "Of course I wouldn't presume to play matchmaker. Why, whatever gave you such an idea? Jennifer is free to bring a friend. Besides, dear, I think Gabriella is a much better catch."

"*Mother!*"

"*Helen!*"

Startled, Chad and Gabriella looked at Helen, at each other, then back at Helen.

"No," Helen continued, undeterred by their outbursts. "You have to choose for yourself, son. Why, I would never interfere where love is concerned. Never."

"*Love.*" Chad shouted.

"Pardon me," Gabriella said. "I think Nina needs to settle in for a nap. If you'll excuse us, I'll take her up now."

Helen relinquished Nina without a struggle. Gabriella didn't like the satisfied smile on the older woman's face.

Love. Humph. Helen was completely wrong. There was nothing remotely resembling love between she and Chad. Absolutely nothing. She wasn't looking for a relationship, and even if she were, he wouldn't be on her list of possibilities. Sure there were moments when they weren't able to take their eyes off each other, and his touch did make her tingle a bit, but surely it wasn't love. Of course not.

Helen didn't know what she was talking about.

****

Gabriella didn't see Chad all day Friday. It wasn't

until they were ready to leave to join the rest of the family on Saturday morning to go hunting for a Christmas tree that he appeared. Dressed in blue jeans, hunting boots, a heavy parka, and knit cap, he looked very rugged indeed. Rugged, and handsome. Gabriella had all she could do to keep her hands tucked in her jacket pockets and her eyes off his piercing blue eyes, his magnetism overpowering.

"You look lovely," he said, coming to her side, taking her arm and leading her toward the front door.

Gabriella gulped at the ease with which he took over—his touch. She wore a red wool sweater, a fleece-lined jacket, and a pair of black leather winter boots. She'd combed her hair back in a braid and twined it in a circle at the nape of her neck so she could put on her red beret-style cap.

"You've got to be kidding. I'm dressed for the outdoors, not a night on the town."

"We'll have to remedy that soon. Shall we go?" he asked.

Who was this man? What was he up to?

So much for his sister's swinging by to pick them up. He opened the car door, made sure she was settled before he circled the Mustang, and got behind the wheel.

"Buckle up."

Gabriella did. But before she could relax, he had the sports car on the move and out of the city winding around the wintry countryside.

"Is there a man in the picture, Gabby? Someone to turn to for help?"

****

"I don't need a man to lean on," she said, startled

by his familiar use of her name, and the bluntness and direction his questioning was taking so quickly. It was true. She'd be just fine once she figured it all out.

"You sound as if you've been hurt. Did someone hurt you?"

"That's none of your business."

It *was* none of his business, yet he made her feel as if it should be, as if he really cared.

"My guess is once this guy found out about Nina he dumped you flat. Bet you scared the pants right off him. Not many men are eager to settle for a ready-made family."

He'd surmised correctly. Was he clairvoyant? This wasn't the first time he'd been able to read her mind. It was getting altogether too disconcerting.

"He never said anything about marriage."

"But he let you down and you don't want to be hurt again?"

She refused to confirm or deny his words.

"What about you? Why aren't you married? I'm sure there are plenty of Jennifers out there who would jump at the chance."

"You asking for the job?"

"No. I told you, I don't need a man in my life right now."

"What? You're not looking for security? A home for Nina? Money?"

He looked at her out of the corner of his eyes. She squirmed.

"You didn't answer *my* question. How come you aren't married like your sisters with a passel of kids of your own?"

The silence in the car stretched before Chad spoke.

"Almost was, but I had a rude awakening," he said, his voice low and angry. "It's no picnic finding out your fiancée is only in it for your money."

Which confirmed what Dennis had said. No wonder he was so hung up on the money issue.

"Please put your mind to rest. I'm neither after you, or your money. I have too many other problems facing me at the moment to worry about getting involved in a relationship going anywhere."

"So you're not interested in a relationship?"

"No way." Her words were quick and emphatic even to her own ears.

"The boyfriend?"

"Boyfriend?"

"Yes, the one who dumped you."

"What about Jennifer?" she shot back, ignoring his question.

"Nope. So, what about the boyfriend? What really happened?"

"Nothing to tell. Like you said, once he found out about Nina, he basically dumped me. End of story. Like Mindy says, I'm better off knowing how Charles feels, now, before we got real serious."

Chad turned onto a side road, and for the next five minutes they climbed, twisted and turned, changed roads again, and in silence, continued to climb even higher until they arrived at a sign announcing Christmas Trees for Sale. Another sign with a picture of a horse and sleigh indicated an old-fashioned treat was in store.

Chad turned onto the long narrow drive. Gabriella spotted Jodi and Sean with their three kids, Sara, Brianna, and Constance, bundled up like chubby penguins against the cold and snow.

Chad smiled at the girls as they ran to the car to greet them. His smile—brilliant, warm and genuine—so different from a few moments ago in the car. It took Gabriella's breath away.

"Look, Uncle Chad," Constance called. "See my new boots."

"Cute, Connie," Chad said, staring at the pink Barbie boots, thinking Connie was too young to be head over heels in love with Barbie stuff, already. He looked at Sara and Brianna who both wore regular boots.

"Where are your Barbie boots?" he asked them.

"That's baby stuff," Sara said, wrinkling her nose.

"Yeah, baby stuff," Brianna mimicked her sister.

"Thank God," Jodi whispered to Gabriella. "I'm glad they're over that craze. Thankfully, Devon is a boy and I won't have to go through that again. Just wait until Nina's a bit older—everything will be Barbie. That babe's young girl appeal never grows old."

Gabriella smiled at the girls. She hadn't even begun to think that far ahead, but it didn't stop the warm motherly feelings starting to fill up the empty places in her heart. Watching Jodi's three kids was a balm to her bruised soul. Instead of emptiness, she had something to look forward to. Something to feel positive about. Being around this family was the best medicine to help heal her heart—their laughter contagious and uplifting.

She smiled. A tummy-warming smile. She and Nina were going to be all right.

Sheila, Jim and their boys were the next to arrive. Everyone waved with excitement, and a second after their car stopped, Jason and Jeffrey jumped from the vehicle and started slinging snowballs at their two uncles—who paid them back without mercy.

"All right," Sheila yelled. "Let's try to keep dry until we at least find our trees. Afterwards you can romp in the snow all you want."

"Can we build a snowman?" Constance asked.

"A whole family of them if you still want to," Jodi told her.

"Come on, brats," Chad called to his nieces and nephews. "Let's go find a sled to get our trees."

Jim had called ahead to make the arrangements so everything was ready to go—no waiting involved. Chad headed for the old carriage house where sleighs and wagons were hooked up to teams of waiting horses and drivers. All five of the children ran toward him. The three girls and three women piled onto one sleigh, and the boys and men on the other, while a third wagon brought up the rear in order to carry the trees back to the parking lot. Red and green plaid blankets were tucked in around everyone's laps and legs, and scarves were wrapped tightly around necks clear up to their noses to ward off the cold.

The gold bells on the horses' braided manes jingled into the crisp mid-morning air as the horses clopped along through the snow-covered hillside toward a stand of trees. Getting into the spirit of the season, the girls started singing *Jingle Bells*, and before long both sleighs filled with tree hunters were bursting with song.

When the horses approached the thicket surrounded in evergreens, the drivers turned them onto a slightly worn path, meandered another five hundred yards, before circling a young grove of evergreens and positioned the wagons to head back downhill.

Without waiting to be told they could get started,

the children jumped from the sleighs and started scouting for their perfect Christmas tree. The adults climbed down from their sleighs more sedately.

"Let us know when you find the trees you want," one of the drivers said. "We'll wait here until you decide." The men pulled out thermoses, poured steaming liquid in the lids, and settled back to wait.

Jodi and Sean caught up with their three girls, while Sheila and Jim curtailed their anxious boys. Which left Gabriella and Chad pairing off together in search of a tree for the Hempstead's home.

Chad followed behind Gabby, her boots making deep indentions in the snow. His mind wandered back to the past week. He'd been busy working on his novel, holed up in his bedroom-turned-office, only coming out when necessary—his story progressing nicely since Jennifer Newell had shown up for drinks. He'd been delighted with the results. At first. But when it came to the femme-fatale character he wanted for Dean Reynolds, the image of Gabriella standing naked, fresh from the shower, kept popping up in his mind, instead. There was just something about her that had him linking Gabby with Dean Reynolds. It kept him frustrated wondering why. Until he finally determined Dean Reynolds bore a striking resemblance to himself.

When the hell had that happened?

While Dean's life was moving right along, Chad's however, was stalled and going nowhere, fast. And, he wasn't sure why. He couldn't stop watching Gabby when she wasn't looking. Like now. She was genuinely warm and caring with his family, and was a loving, devoted mother to her niece. The little tyke was getting to him, too, and a couple of times he caught himself wanting to pick her up and hold her. Where that urge had come from, he had no idea. He shook his head and continued traipsing behind her.

Gabby on the other hand, didn't appear to be too broken hearted over this Charles character. If on the rebound, she wouldn't have admitted she was glad he dumped her. But it didn't explain why *he* was beginning to care. Or why he should care if Charles had dumped her and left her with a baby to care for all on her own. Why should he care if Dennis took her to dinner while he stayed home and stewed? He simply cared. And, he had to admit he liked the warm cozy feelings he got every time she was near.

Chad took a deep breath and discovered the heady scent of crisp, clean, country air mingled with pine and snow. A hint of horse odors reminiscent of his youth surrounded him—the horses' whinnies, the steam from their nostrils shot into the clear morning air, and the jingle of the bells hanging around their necks tinkled melodiously. As a child, he'd spent many summers at his grandparents' horse farm in central New York. But like many other farmers these days, their children, like Chad's father, chose a different vocation. His grandparents retired, sold the place, and moved south. Chad missed those summer visits.

He longed for those happier days. Damn, he was feeling sappy again. *'Tis the season.*

What would he do with a horse now?

"This one. This one. It's the biggest," Jeffrey yelled to his parents.

"No. No," Jason called back. "This one over here. It's taller."

On the other side of the trail, Gabriella trudged

through the snow, circling one tree after another. Chad had a strong urge to grab her hand and wrap his arm around her to protect her from the cold. She stood back, looked a tree up and down, the way he was looking at her now.

The temperature shot up a notch.

She chewed the corner of her lower lip as if she were contemplating the biggest decision of her life. He wanted to place his lips on hers. Help her decide.

The heat surrounding him soared higher.

Chad wiped the sweat from his forehead. Hell. What was it about this woman that had him reacting like a teenager every time they were together? It was getting worse day by day. He had to break the spell or he'd go mad.

He wondered if she liked horses.

Chapter Eight

"You're not seeing anyone at the moment?" Chad asked again, unexpectedly. "What about Dennis? Is something going on between the two of you?"

Chad was persistent, if nothing else.

Gabriella took a deep breath, looked up into his dreamy blue eyes, and felt her stomach bunch. She pivoted in the snow, needing to put distance between them. She circled another tree. Her arm brushed against one of the elongated branches, the movement causing a cascade of snow to flurry and plunk to the ground. She heard Chad cuss under his breath and knew he'd received a cold shower.

Gabriella continued until she came to another tree. She stopped to check it out before she dare look at him again. "What difference does it make?" She finally answered on a sigh, and moved on to circle another snow-covered tree. This time she was careful not to brush against it, knowing he was hot on her heels.

"Just answer the question, dammit," he bit out, clearly frustrated.

"It's none of your business." She moved past a large tree to their left, looked it up and down and decided it was the perfect tree. Once it was decorated, it would be magnificent.

He followed and stopped beside her.

"It's a simple question. Yes or no?"

Cocooned in the dense hillside, white covered pines and green spruce boughs softened their voices. In a world of their own where there were no sounds of children, or the whinny of horses. No tinkles of sleigh bells. The breeze stood still. The scent of evergreens heavy in the air. Wrapped in a winter wonderland, they were suspended in time.

"No," she said. "There is no relationship. I have my hands full at the moment."

He smiled. "What about Dennis?"

He stood much too close—their surroundings stirring her emotions. Her heart did a somersault.

Plop. Plop, plop, plop.

Snowballs landed on Chad's back, and before Gabriella could duck out of the way, the entire family descended on them. They were fully involved in a very serious snowball fight. It was hard to determine who was on whose side. Ten minutes later the lines were clearly drawn—girls against boys, men against women.

After being unmercifully bombarded by the men, Gabriella had had enough. Armed with several slightly packed weapons, she rushed out from behind a small spruce and rushed the enemy lines. Chad took retreat, and after passing several small trees, ducked behind a larger evergreen. Gabriella easily followed his footprints in the snow—his laughter a dead giveaway. When she rushed around the tree, arm raised, Chad was right there blocking her aim. His arm caught hers, forcing her to drop her weapon, which landed on top of his head. The snowball broke apart and avalanched down his face.

Without holding back, Gabriella laughed. And laughed. Lord, she hadn't had much to laugh about lately, and she couldn't stop. She laughed so hard at the stunned look on Chad's face with snow melting down his forehead and over his long, dark eyelashes, onto his cheeks. Tears rolled down her own face.

Tenderly, he cupped her cheeks and wiped her tears of laughter away with his thumbs. She stopped laughing and looked deep into his eyes. His touch mesmerized her. Her heart stopped beating, then wound tight into overdrive with a wild thudding that droned in her ears. Lightheaded, she clasped his wrists for support. It was a warm, comfortable mistake. He stepped forward.

And kissed her.

She responded, leaning into his embrace.

Chad deepened the kiss. His arms circled her neck, and waist, the barrier of their winter clothes no obstacle.

Chad's kiss produced enough heat to melt the entire North Pole. Gabriella's body grew limp. Drowning in a sea of heavenly bliss, she gave in to the sensations only to have reality hit in the form of another barrage of snowballs with cries of "got ya" and much yelling and laughing.

Chad broke the contact, swirled around, dipped his hand in the snow to fling a snowball at the intruders so fast Gabriella lost her balance and fell into the snow— flat on her back. She lay stunned, eyes shut. A warm breath whispered across her cheek. She opened her eyes to find Constance standing over her.

"What are you doing down there? Why are you laying in the snow?"

Gabriella looked into Constance's quizzical face and all the wonderful memories of growing up with her own family made her smile.

"Making a snow angel," she said. "Do you know how to make them?"

Constance shook her head.

"Here, let me show you."

Gabriella proceeded to move her arms up and down in the snow, and her legs from side to side. When she got up to show Constance the angel image she had made, Chad was right there to give her a hand up so she wouldn't damage the impression.

"Wow," Constance stared at the large shape of a Christmas angel. "Can I make one, too?"

"Sure," Chad said. He lifted her up in the air and placed her on her back in the snow, away from their footprints.

Before long everyone, including the grownups, lay in the snow quietly making snow angels.

"See what you started," Chad said. He lay in the snow next to her, swinging his arms and legs back and forth in a flapping motion. "I haven't done this since I was a kid. I forgot how much fun it is playing in the snow. Can't remember the last time I had a good snowball fight, either."

"You've been grown up for far too long," Gabriella said. "Nothing like children around to remind you what fun is all about. Especially at holiday time."

"Has it been so hard for you, having a baby to take care of on your own?"

"They certainly change your life and can turn it upside down," Gabriella said with much more sadness than she had intended. "But I don't want your sympathy, so take that 'I feel sorry for you' look off your face."

Gabriella jumped up and brushed her backside off. "This tree, I think," she said, pointing to the ten-foot blue spruce in front of her. "It will look great in your parents' library."

Amidst much laughter and more snow flying about, trees were cut and placed in the wagons. The sleighs headed down the hillside with much singing and more laughter echoing the hillside. It started to snow. Big, lazy, drifting flakes landed on Gabriella's nose and eyelashes. She huddled under the blanket and tried not to think about Chad's kiss. It was impossible. No one had ever kissed her quite the way he did. She couldn't remember ever responding in such abandon, either. She didn't want to feel anything for Chad Hempstead, but she did. In a matter of weeks he'd be gone without a backward glance.

****

Everyone congregated at the Hempsteads' and stayed to help trim the tree. The three men managed to get it set up and steady in the corner of the room away from the fireplace so it wouldn't dry out from the heat. In the meantime, Chadwick had gone to the attic and retrieved the decorations. Ethel brought in the tree skirt, and along with Helen, they settled in to play with the babies—Devon and Nina. The cousins delighted in helping the grownups dig through the decorations, oohing and aahing over each one they unwrapped before running to the tree to hang it on a bare branch. Amongst the chaos someone started singing Christmas Carols. The room filled with high holiday spirits. Gabriella couldn't help but be blessed to be surrounded with such love so soon after the loss of her own family. And for Nina to be included as if she belonged.

The miracle of family was overwhelming. If only for a short time, she was going to enjoy every second.

Nina's sudden burst of crying had everyone turning to see what was wrong. Chad ran to her side. Gabriella couldn't believe the look of concern written all over his face once again. Before she could circle around the tree to see what was wrong, Chad bent over the bassinet, retrieved the pink pacifier and inserted it in the crying baby's mouth. He stood for a moment longer as if to make sure she was okay.

"Chad," his mother called from across the room. "Bring that lovely child over here to me so I can hold her. She might have a bubble needing to come up."

The expression on Chad's face changed from concern to panic. Had he never held or picked up a baby before? He looked startled, terrified. She started to go to his rescue when Sheila put her hand on Gabriella's shoulder.

"Let me. It's about time he learned how this is done," Sheila whispered and went to her brother's side. "Here, hold your arms like this," she instructed, positioning his arms ready to receive the baby. Sheila picked Nina up and smiled as she placed her in Chad's waiting arms. "It's not so bad, is it?"

Chad looked stunned. He didn't utter a word but carefully walked across the floor with Nina in his arms. He placed the infant in his mother's lap, expelled the breath he'd been holding in a loud whoosh. The men laughed, taking turns patting him on the shoulder. Gabriella couldn't help but smile at the look of satisfaction on his face. Anyone would think he'd won first prize in a sporting event.

"You did fine, Son." Helen smiled up at him.

Chad looked at Gabriella. Her heart stopped. His look was one of emotional bonding, of wonder, admiration, and understanding. A look lasting no longer than a moment, but full of meaning, warmth. Gabriella's knees weakened.

Tree-trimming continued. Garland, tinsel, ornaments, and bells were strewn everywhere as decorations continued to be lifted reverently from their boxes and placed just as caringly on the tree. Several times Gabriella caught Chad watching her, and twice he put his hands on her shoulders to move her out of his way so he could hang an ornament on one of the higher branches. Each time he touched her, an electric current shot down her arms clear to her fingertips. Twice, she almost dropped a glass ornament.

An hour later the tree was trimmed, looking professionally decorated. Ethel gave Devon to his mother, then wheeled the tea trolley in, laden with an assortment of homemade cookies and confections. There was hot cocoa for the children.

Gabriella's spirits soared. What a perfect day.

****

Gabriella had hoped to be excluded from the evening's social later that night, but Helen would hear none of it.

"It's not as if I'm family, Helen. You've been too gracious already. You and Ethel have been fabulous with Nina, too. I'm very grateful."

"We love having you here, my dear. Now, why don't you have a rest while Nina is sleeping, and we'll see you this evening."

Truth be told, Gabriella couldn't be more at home and feel part of the Hempstead household. The two women had taken to Nina just as if she were one of their own granddaughters. They were regular mother hens. And she was starting to wish she could stay here forever. And that would never do.

Nina had just closed her eyes and was sleeping soundly when Ethel knocked on her door and stuck her head inside the room. "You have a call. A Mindy Crandall. Says she's a friend of yours."

"Yes. She's my roommate."

"I brought the kitchen phone up for you to use. Just take it back down when you're finished."

Gabriella took the phone over to the bed and settled against the pillows. She hadn't talked to Mindy since Wednesday night. She'd been surprised to learn her friend had postponed going home for break. She hoped nothing was wrong.

The two exchanged the usual greetings before Mindy got down to business.

"I got a call from your brother-in-law's lawyer. He's been trying to locate you. Something about a trust fund for Nina. He wants you to call him this afternoon. Said he'd be in all evening."

"But it's Saturday."

"What can I say? The guy must not have a life. I hope it's good news. By the way, how's it going with Mr. Mustang?"

"Like Dennis said, he's not so bad once you get to know him."

"Am I hearing a bit of interest in him in the tone of your voice?"

"No." Gabriella effectively squelched the topic of Chad by telling her about the family excitement over the tree. No way was she ready to tell Mindy about the

127

kiss.

"I thought you'd be on your way home by now. What's going on?"

"Nothing much. Trish finished her labs and exams. She didn't leave until yesterday. Said to say bye, and hope you're doing okay. She misses Nina."

"You have a safe trip home. Have a great holiday with the family. I'll see you when you get back after the break."

"Gabby?"

"Yeah?"

"Be happy."

****

After calling the lawyer back, Gabriella hung up the phone in pleased dismay. Tom had set up a trust fund for Nina when she was born. The lawyer had only recently worked through the details and had been trying to contact her. To Gabriella's astonishment, the money was being made available immediately under the guardianship of none other than Gabriella, herself. All she had to do was sign on the dotted lines. To expedite matters, the lawyer was going to send the paperwork to her via overnight mail.

Gabriella's financial worries in regards to the care of Nina were over. With a trust fund and eventually the life insurance, now all she had to do was obtain legal custody. She could withdraw the Leave-of-Absence forms and finish her degree, as planned.

More lighthearted than she'd been in a long time, Gabriella did a dance around the room, sent up a silent prayer of thanks, and took the phone back downstairs.

****

Gabriella entered the library that evening, a smile

on her face, her spirits high, ready to enjoy the evening without a worry on her mind, and froze. Charles Denton, on the arm of Jennifer Newell was a shock she could have lived without. Once she got over the initial bombshell, her first thought was she and Nina had had a narrow escape.

She cringed at his triumphant smile. What was he doing here? And with Jennifer Newell? Glancing around the room, hoping her anxiety didn't show, Gabriella didn't want anyone to discover her connection with Charles. But when her eyes met Chad's, a split second was all it took for Charles to put two and two together and come up with his own sordid and wrong conclusions.

Charles, Jennifer still on his arm, made his way to her side.

"Hello, Ella. Looks like you landed on your feet."

Gabriella bristled at his familiar use of her name— liking instead the shortened version of Gabby that Chad used. Ella was more formal and uncomfortable, especially coming from Charles' lips.

"Ella? The two of you know each other?" Chad asked.

Gabriella was taken aback at how fast Chad had made it to her side. His closeness was somehow comforting.

"Yes. This is Charles Denton, an acquaintance of mine from university. Charles this is Chad Hempstead."

Gabriella's hands shook, her voice wobbled. She wanted to kick herself for her outward discomfort. God only knew what Charles was thinking, especially after his comment. Had Chad heard it?

"And we've already met," Jennifer quipped, and

stepped forward, not to be ignored.

No one paid her any attention.

"What brings you here, Denton?" Chad questioned.

"Jen invited me. That a problem, Hempstead?"

The two squared off. Gabriella's head swiveled from one to the other. Chad looked at Gabriella. Gabriella wished she was anywhere else but standing between these two men. Unable to escape the uncomfortable situation without being overly rude, she focused instead on the winter twilight streaming in through the window—the full moon making its evening journey across the starry sky. She found herself comparing Chad to Charles and discovered there really was no comparison. Charles just didn't measure up. What had she ever seen in him? Although Chad had been cautious around his nieces and nephews, he had genuinely enjoyed their company all day. She found Chad to be thoughtful of others, caring of his parents, fun to be around, and patient with children. Including Nina.

Not to mention his kisses were way more enjoyable than Charles' had ever been. How had she considered Charles' chaste kisses a sign of love and a happily-ever-after? Chad might have been suspicious, but now that she understood why, she didn't blame him for acting cautious and concerned when he'd discovered her in his parents' home. He was only trying to protect his family—and his heart. For some reason this revelation warmed her soul from her heart clear down to her toes. Chad was more of a family man than he cared to admit. She couldn't wait to tell him her financial woes were a thing of the past. See where their relationship might lead.

"Hello, Jennifer. Who's your friend," Sheila asked.

Sheila, Jodi and their husbands had arrived, breaking the spell between the two men, and her contemplations. She really had to get control of her emotions. Flight was upper most in her mind. Jennifer preened her hair, pasted a sickening smile on her face and proceeded to take front and center.

"My friend is none other than Charles Denton— *The* Boston Dentons," she gushed. "Our families have known each other forever. We go way back, don't we, Denny?"

Gabriella gulped. Denny? Really?

Charles didn't bat an eye at the familiarity of Jennifer calling him what was most likely a childhood name. In fact, he ignored her and instead extended his hand to Sean and Jim in greeting. Gabriella noticed that he hadn't done the same for Chad. But then, Chad hadn't offered his hand either.

Gabriella wished that the baby monitor would go off so she could escape this dreadful and most awkward situation.

As the evening progressed, however, Gabriella found herself watching Charles from the corner of her eyes. What was he really doing at the Hempsteads? Was it simply a coincidence? Or was it Jennifer's plan to make Chad jealous? It didn't matter—she didn't trust either of them.

Sheila and Jodi put two and two together and kept her occupied in conversation like two mother hens. At one point, they managed to drift off to greet other family friends. Gabriella stood just inside the hallway alcove admiring the holiday scene. The women sat next to the hearth with the fire crackling behind them, and the men stood in varying poses around their women folk, drinks in hand. The Christmas tree filled one whole corner of the room, the lights sparkling off the shiny ornaments, while soft holiday music played in the background. Able to finally relax for the first time since entering the library, she took a deep breath. Everyone was socializing. No one would miss her. It was the perfect time to slip away.

A movement to her left caught her attention.

"Alone at last," Charles said.

The sneer in his tone put her on alert, his cold eyes bored into hers. He reached for her, drew her into his arms, his face inches from hers. She panicked, shoved against his chest, but his arms had locked around her so tight she couldn't move.

"Relax," he said.

His alcohol-saturated breath assailed her. She cringed. Was Charles drunk? She'd never seen him like this before. They'd shared a glass of wine over dinner on occasion, but Charles had always been careful not to let her over indulge.

"You were never afraid of my touch before," he snarled, crushing her closer.

She gasped. *Lord, what did I ever see in this man— what made me think I was in love with him?*

Not wanting to make a scene, she kept her tone level.

"Let me go, Charles. You're here with Jennifer. What is it you want? What are you trying to prove?"

"Leave Jen out of this. This is between you and me. We have unfinished business."

"Have you changed your mind about Nina?"

"No. But I'm sure we can work things out."

"I'm not changing my mind."

"How are you going to cope? Don't you need my money? Hempstead offer a better financial deal?"

"I don't need anyone's money. A trust fund was set up—between that and the life insurance policy that will eventually be available, all Nina's needs will be covered."

Gabriella tried to squirm out of his hold.

"Well, whaddya know," he slurred. "Mistletoe. How convenient. Bet you were just waiting for me here, huh, Ella? Well, I'm here now, babe. What are we waiting for?"

Babe? If she weren't so upset over Charles' behavior, his words would have been laughable. For him to think she was still interested and wanted to kiss him—mistletoe or no mistletoe—was ludicrous. And he had to be drunk to think she'd waited just for him to notice she was standing under the mistletoe.

Keeping her voice low, but loud enough for him to understand, she tried once more to get him to release his hold.

"You gave up all rights of kissing me when you all but told me to 'kiss off,' Charles. Remember? Now, let me go."

She tried again to pry herself away from him.

"For the record," Gabriella continued, "I made the right choice. You did me a huge favor. I have no idea why you think I'd want you back. I still have Nina. Did you think your rejection of her would impact my decision to keep her?" His hold loosened slightly. Gabriella took advantage and turned away.

"Not so fast," he snapped, and swung her back against his chest. "We have unfinished business."

"No. We. Don't. We're finished, Charles. I suggest you go find Jennifer and ask her to take you home. You're drunk." Gabriella didn't know what he was trying to prove, but she didn't care. He was making a spectacle of them in front of the Hempsteads.

"I can see you're after more than I was willing to hand out," Charles grinned, undeterred. "I see the way you look at Hempstead. He doesn't like gold-diggers, Babe. Once he finds out you're only after his money, he'll dump you so fast you'll wonder what happened."

"Unlike you, of course. I told you I don't need anyone's money."

"You really don't know who Chad Hempstead is, do you?"

"I notice you know Miss Newell well enough," Gabriella raised her eyebrows and continued. "It didn't take you long to find someone else."

"Leave Jen out of this," he hissed between clenched teeth.

It crossed Gabriella's mind that perhaps Charles and Jennifer had been an item at one time, perhaps they still were.

"Gladly. Now if you'll excuse me, I think we have nothing more to say to each other."

His grip on her loosened, and this time Gabriella was able to break free.

Although heated, their argument was achieved in low tones. Gabriella was pleased to note she was able to break away without causing a major scene.

But she hadn't counted on his drunken state, or anticipated his actions.

"Oh, but we have a lot more to say," he said in a much louder tone.

Gabriella looked behind her and was dismayed to see he had drawn attention to their argument, after all.

"I think not," she said, keeping her own voice low, hoping he'd do the same. "You've shown me the kind of person you really are, Charles. And it was never a matter of money."

"No?" Charles asked, raising an eyebrow. "Not about money? Then why are you here making lovesick eyes at Hempstead? Your chances with Mr. Celebrity won't get you very far once he finds out you're after his money."

"I don't know what you're talking about, and I don't care. Now if you'll excuse me, I'm going to join the others."

Charles grabbed her and wrapped his arms around her waist—this time his lips descended, finding their unwilling mark. Repulsed, Gabriella froze. She shoved at him—he tumbled backwards into the doorframe. She glared at him with a sense of overwhelming loathing and shame that she'd ever considered herself in love with Charles. She turned to walk away and was drawn into a strong, comforting pair of arms. Stunned, she looked up into Chad's cold blue eyes now glaring at Charles.

"I think you owe Gabby an apology, Denton."

"A mistletoe kiss doesn't warrant an apology, Hempstead," he slurred. "Mind your own business."

"Gabby is a guest in our home, so that makes her my business. Take care, Denton. It's clear you've blown your chances when you broke it off with Gabby."

"Broke it off? You've got it all wrong, Hempstead. She chose her sister's baby over me."

"Good choice. Now be a good boy and move on."

Charles glared at Gabriella, a snarl distorting his otherwise handsome features. "You're welcome to her and her baggage. As long as you have enough money to support them, they'll be in the palm of your hands."

"Shut up, Denton. Say another word and you'll be sorry."

So much for not making a scene. Gabriella scanned the room and was appalled to see everyone watching the trio under the mistletoe. She wanted to lay a finger aside of her nose and disappear up the chimney into a puff of smoke. Lord, to have those carefree days of only a few months ago would be heaven. She was exhausted from trying to keep up with everything, and now this.

"She's only after your money, Hempstead. How's that for a kick in the pants?"

Chad raised his arm and punched Charles in the nose. Gabriella gasped at the loud crack resounding around the library just before Charles landed against the wall and slid to the floor. Her gasp was nothing compared to the sound of the collective gasps behind her. Transfixed by the sight of the now oozing dark-red blood flowing from the middle of Charles' face, Gabriella was further dismayed when Jennifer, as if in slow motion, rushed to his side, plucking tissues from her handbag to mop up the blood. Charles untangled himself and stood like the drunk he was. From out of nowhere, Dennis appeared at Gabriella's side, his arm circling her shoulders in comfort. Chad turned to the two of them, anger still evident in the cold glare of his expressive eyes.

"Touch her, Long, and you'll get the same."

"Calm down, Buddy. You're acting just like Dean

Reynolds. She just needs a comforting arm right now and I don't think you're showing any restraint at the moment."

"Dean Reynolds?" Gabriella asked. She looked from Chad to Dennis. "Who's Dean Reynolds?"

Was that a giggle she heard coming from the direction of Sheila and Jodi?

"Oh, he's a real character," Sheila said, the humor in her voice puzzling Gabriella.

The angry glare Chad directed at his sisters was even more puzzling. Just who was this Dean Reynolds character?

Chapter Nine

Every eye in the room focused on Gabriella in the now crowded alcove. Jennifer Newell shot livid daggers her way. The others, not quite knowing what had just transpired to cause Chad to punch Charles in the nose, stood gawking at the scene unfolding. Jodi and Sheila's grins didn't make any sense. And Helen, God love her, looked giddier than a schoolgirl on her first date—she absolutely beamed. Gabby wanted to sink into the woodwork.

Jennifer wrapped her arm through Charles', and tried without much success, to tug him to her side. "Oh, my poor darling. Let me help," she all but simpered.

"Shut up, Jen," Charles snapped, his teeth clamped together. "Leave me alone." He pushed her aside, but Jennifer held strong a moment longer before giving up, only to turn on Gabriella.

"You!" she spat. "This is all your fault." Jennifer swung her head from Gabriella to Charles and back again. "Oh. My. God. Charles. Of course. You're the father of her baby, aren't you? That's it. We're through," she hissed between clenched pearly white teeth framed in a deep red that perfectly matched Charles' still oozing blood. "I'm out of here. Chad, take me home."

"Wait. Jen. There's no need to get upset," Charles tried to soothe the distraught Jennifer. "That baby is not mine. It's not hers, either. It's her sister's. Come on, *I'll* take you home."

"You're in no shape to drive," she said.

Gabriella had to hand it to Jennifer. She staunchly turned her back on Charles. Shoulders drawn back, head held high, she walked off leaving him in shocked disbelief.

Charles sneered at Gabriella—if looks could kill. He stalked off, following Jennifer. Gabriella's eyes connected with Chad's. His smile was tentative. He nodded, then followed Charles—as did Dennis. Left alone, not knowing what to make of it all, Gabriella turned in the other direction and approached the Hempsteads.

"I'm so sorry, Helen, Chadwick. I'm afraid it *was* all my fault. I didn't mean to ruin your party."

"Nonsense, my dear," Helen said. "It wasn't your fault at all. Mr. Denton had no reason to accost you. Why, I witnessed the whole thing."

Gabriella noted the hint of a smile on Helen's serious face and was reminded of Jodi and Sheila's giggles.

"Why don't you call it a night and go get some rest. I'm sure the men will work it all out."

As Gabriella attempted to leave, Jodi and Sheila were right behind her.

"Are you all right?" Jodi asked.

Both women looked at her with concern.

"I'm fine. Really," Gabriella shakily assured them.

"Sorry, we didn't mean to desert you. We had no idea Charles would purposely set out to humiliate you in front of everyone," Sheila said.

"I don't think anyone expected Chad to punch him

in the nose, either." Jodi smiled. "My opinion of my brother just moved up a notch. I think he ranks right up there with Dean."

"Dean?" Gabriella asked. "Who's this Mr. Reynolds?"

"Oh. Oh, my. No one," Sheila stuttered. "Is that Nina I hear?"

Gabriella glanced up, concerned. "I'd better go get her bottle and check on her."

She wanted nothing more than to kick off her shoes, fall into bed, and call it a night, as Helen suggested. She looked at Chad's sisters and smiled.

"I am actually tired. And it's almost time for Nina's last feeding for the night. If you'll excuse me."

Gabriella paused a moment longer.

"Am I missing something?"

"Well…ahem…we did see you and Chad kissing this morning when we were tree-hunting. Our lips are sealed though." Their smiles were wide and knowing.

"Sheila, Jodi… I…what are…"

"I think you've had enough excitement for one day. What do you think, Jodi, our lips are sealed, right?"

"Yep. The folks won't hear a word from us. 'Course the children might have seen you and Chad kissing, too. They aren't exactly secret-keepers—they love to share everything at the most inopportune moments. You never know what kids will say."

"Listen, you two, there is absolutely nothing going on between me and your brother."

"Yeah, right. Chad just punched Charles in the nose for the fun of it. Sure, like I believe that."

The two sisters chuckled as they returned to the library. Gabriella's face burned.

"Those two are as bad as their mother," Gabriella whispered as sounds of more giggles followed her up the stairs.

****

There was no way he was about to apologize for punching Charles Denton in the nose. He did owe his parents an apology for creating a scene, although it was a struggle to apologize for something he really wasn't sorry about. He was glad. The jerk had it coming, man-handling Gabby like that—kissing her. Mistletoe or no mistletoe, it was obvious she hadn't wanted to be kissed.

Dean Reynolds would have done the same.

He was, however, sorry he'd upset Gabby, although she'd looked more stunned than angry when Denton landed against the wall with blood dripping down his chin. And he owed Dennis an apology. Hell, he was only trying to be helpful. And he was grateful that his friend had stepped in and offered to take Jennifer home while he called a cab for Charles. For one thing, he didn't want Jennifer to get the wrong idea. He might feel sorry for her, but no way was he going to get tangled up with her. Dennis could take care of himself.

Chad couldn't stop thinking about Gabriella—their *shared* kiss next to the snow-covered spruce with white fluffy flakes drifting in the crisp afternoon air. A winter wonderland that warmed every inch of his aroused body. And it was a shared kiss—the sparks igniting between the two of them were definitely mutual. He'd wanted to get her under the mistletoe all evening in order to have an excuse to steal another kiss, but that damn Charles Denton had beaten him to it.

Needing to cool off before he exploded, he grabbed his winter jacket, stuffed his arms through the sleeves and wrapped his scarf securely around his neck. He headed out the door. He dug for his gloves—they weren't in his pockets. The hell with them. He didn't need them anyway. He headed toward the gazebo.

Had he been a fool? Was Gabriella after his money as Charles suggested? He'd planned to tell her about his writing—come clean. Now, he wasn't so sure it was the right thing to do. *Ah, damn!* He should never have come home for the holidays. His life was becoming more messed up than Dean's. The minute he'd laid eyes on Gabby he'd had a premonition something bigger and more powerful than his mother's matchmaking was at work.

He'd need a miracle to untangle his emotions and get out of this mess with his sanity still intact.

****

By the time Nina settled back to sleep, all the guests had left and a silent peacefulness blanketed the Hempstead's home once more. Gabriella was wide-awake after resting, and decided to go to the kitchen to get a cup of tea and some of Ethel's holiday treats to take back to the library where she could relax next to what was left of the fire. She ran a brush through her hair, slipped into her white terry robe, and tightened the belt. She slipped on a pair of warm, fuzzy slipper-socks and quietly shut the door and tiptoed down the hallway.

She'd been on edge ever since her sister's accident, and had finally started to enjoy being a mother. Staying at the Hempstead's had helped. She was happier than she'd been in a long time. Still, the incident with Charles tonight had left her emotions raw and in shambles.

The day had started out so well, only going downhill when Charles arrived. And ending with Chad punching Charles in the nose. She was glad the incident hadn't blown into a full-scale fistfight. She'd never be able to show her face again if it had come to that.

A few embers glowed in the grate, and the smell of apple wood filled the room. Gabriella set her cup and plate of cookies down on the end table, and settled back in the plush cushions. She smiled to herself, resting her head on one of the throw pillows.

The lights were low, and even though the tree lights had been unplugged, the full moon shone through the window. A magical peace filled the room. Something about the coziness of the muted sights and sounds of the night wrapped around her like a protective, warm, secure blanket. A feeling of belonging, of being home made her think of her parents and sister. She missed them all so much.

Restless, Gabriella walked to the window and gazed at the winter wonderland outside. The lake was partially frozen. Lights twinkled on either side of the snow-covered shores, their glow sparkled on the water. With a deep sigh, she turned and crossed the room to the bookshelves.

Gabriella was surprised at the Hempstead's eclectic selection. Along with classics, business, law, and even children's books, she was intrigued by the large collection by an author named Bronson B. Brady. After perusing the titles, Gabriella discovered Mr. Hempstead was fond of these detective novels.

She had just chosen one of the many books lining the middle shelf—*Detective Dean Reynolds: On Ice*—

when she remembered Dennis had said Chad had been acting just like Dean Reynolds. So had Chad's sisters. Book in hand, Gabriella went back to her chair. About to settle in for a good read, she was startled when Chad entered the room. He looked near froze to death from the cold, and her newly acquired motherly instincts kicked in. She ran to his side at the same time he started toward the warmth of the fire. Almost colliding, they stopped in front of each other. Chad placed his hands on her shoulders to steady her.

"Your hands are freezing," she said.

"I've been for a walk."

"In this weather?" She clutched the book she held in both hands against her chest. His hands might be cold, but the heat emanating from his body made the glowing embers in the fireplace flicker no warmer than a candle. Her eyes smoldered, but before she could guess at his intentions, she was in his arms. Chad's lips locked possessively over hers, his strong arms circling her waist. He kissed her as if he couldn't get enough of her.

Caught up in the moment, Gabriella let the book slip from her hands onto the carpet. It landed with a soft thud.

Gabriella's feet rose from the floor as Chad lifted her in the air and swirled her around like a music-box dancer. As they slowed, the silent music entwining them reached an end—their breaths mingled, drawing sustaining life from each other. Their hearts beat in unison, a symphony only the two of them shared. Chad held her secure in his embrace, their lips still clinging. Slowly, Gabriella slid down Chad's now hot, taut body, feeling every muscle, every… everything until the tips of her toes made contact with the carpet once again. She rested her forehead on his chest and listened to his heartbeat... or was it hers? She couldn't tell. Chad's chin rested on top of her head, his breath teasing her hair. She turned her cheek into his chest, smelled the fresh outdoors, and blinked back to the present. She didn't want the magical spell to end. She simply wanted to stay in his arms forever. She had finally come home. Safe. Secure. Loved?

Chad swayed with Gabriella in his arms. Having to let go was the most abysmal idea in the world. Everything about this woman turned his preconceived images of love upside-down. He didn't know where they were headed, but he had to tell his mother to stop matchmaking already. He could handle things just fine all on his own.

"Who needs mistletoe?" he whispered, and putting his fingers under her chin, lifted her face to his. His own feelings of longing were reflected in her eyes. He couldn't resist kissing her again. But when he leaned toward her, his foot kicked something on the floor. He looked down and found his face staring up at him from the back cover of one of his books Gabriella had been holding. Glancing back at Gabriella, her eyes closed, waiting for his kiss, he saw red. He'd been a fool once again. Thankfully, the trust fund he'd secretly arranged for Nina had stipulations. He'd chided himself for being so cautious when his lawyer had suggested the cautionary measures. It's a good thing he hadn't listened to his heart after all.

Gabriella stumbled forward, losing her balance. The two of them tumbled to the floor and the book skirted across the room.

"Ah," he said, and reached down to retrieve it. "An interesting choice. Why this one in particular? The author, perhaps?"

The author? Gabriella wasn't sure what he was getting at. Chad's tone, while soft and seductive, held a hint of something else that belied his suggestiveness. What did reading the book by Bronson B. Brady have to do with anything?

"I...I don't know what you mean," Gabriella stuttered softy, trying to get up. "I came down for tea and wanted something to read."

"So you picked that book? Do you know the author, hmmm...?"

"No. No, I don't. I just found several here. They looked interesting. I've got to admit the name Dean Reynolds piqued my interest after Dennis and your sisters commented on it earlier."

"My sisters? What did they tell you? What about Dean Reynolds?"

"Nothing. They just said he was a character. I didn't realize he was a character in a book until I spotted it on the shelf. I decided to read one and find out for myself, seeing as no one was willing to tell me anything."

"Tell me, why did Charles say you were after my money?"

"Why does Charles say anything? I don't know— maybe because I asked him for a small loan and he turned me down. But it isn't true. I told you before, I don't need anyone's money."

"So you say. Why would he mention it if it wasn't true? I was right about you all along, wasn't I?"

Gabriella bristled. Her eyes narrowed.

"I thought we got beyond this. Apparently I was wrong."

Chad handed her the book, his picture staring back from the back cover.

"It's you." She smiled in amazement. "Oh, my God. Chad. That's you! I can't believe it. You're the author!"

"You knew. Of course you knew," he stated. "You couldn't have Charles, so you settled on making a grab for me? You waited up for me and my money tonight and made it look like a chance meeting."

"What are you talking about?" Gabriella stared at him as if he had two heads—she was in the Twilight Zone. She steadied her shaky legs and brushed her hands down the side of her robe to stop them from trembling.

"I had no idea. No one ever said." Wow. Chad was Bronson B. Brady and Dean Reynolds was a character in his books. There were a number of his books lining the shelf. He must be famous. And wealthy. No wonder he accused her of being after his money.

Her robe had come undone from their tumble on the floor. She tightened the belt, brushed the hair back from her face, and didn't give a damn if her socks had slipped off her feet during their earth-shattering kiss. She felt cheapened, insulted, and close to tears.

Angrier than she had ever been before, even when Charles had dumped her, Gabriella exploded. She might be a fool once for thinking she was in love with Charles, but she wasn't going to be caught a second time. Especially by someone who accused her of being after his money. Apparently, Chad hadn't gotten past that point. Had he been manipulating her all this time waiting to see if she would slip up so he could prove she was like all the other women that were after his money?

"First of all," she said, catching her breath and letting it out in a rush. "Do I look like I'm dressed for seduction? Second of all, I don't know who Bronson B. Brady is, but I do know Chadwick Hempstead, Jr. And from where I'm standing he isn't much of a catch."

"Maybe not, but I have the bank account that reels them in."

Gabriella's arm flew foreword, the flat of her palm connecting with Chad's cheek before she could call it back. The loud crack filled the silent room, sounding an awful lot like the embers popping in the fireplace. But she wasn't about to apologize. Or be humiliated again.

"I trusted you. I thought you really cared for me. But I guess I was wrong. Again."

Chad stood silent.

"I don't get *reeled in*, and I never check anyone's bank accounts before I let them kiss me. And I don't need to stand here and be insulted by you. For the last time, I don't need your money. Hell, I don't even need this job any longer. A trust has been set up for Nina, so she's no longer the burden everyone seems to think."

Beyond tears, Gabriella no longer needed or wanted a book to read. She skirted around Chad, stopped in the doorway, turned back, and found his face ashen, sporting a red mark on his left cheek where her hand had connected.

"You need to figure out what the important things in life are, Junior. Grow up. Not everyone is after your money."

****

148

Gabriella refused to cry. She lay on top of the bedcovers, eyes closed. An errant tear trickled from the corner of her eyelid. Wiping it away would only acknowledge it. She wouldn't cry over Chad Hempstead/Bronson B. Brady no matter how devastated she was to realize she had fallen in love with him. He didn't trust her with who he was. And she wasn't going to acknowledge she had just admitted she had fallen in love with him. *Fool!*

Another tear trickled down Gabriella's cheek, making its way slowly down her face, landing next to her ear, seeping silently into the pillow. Gabriella squeezed her eyes shut. Her hands lay limp at her sides.

She refused to cry.

****

Not sure what had just happened, Chad plunked down on the easy chair Gabriella had been sitting in next to the fire. What he did know was their kiss had been one hellava kiss and it had shaken him up more than he'd care to admit. He hadn't meant to turn against Gabby. *Damn.* Hearing Charles call Gabby a gold-digger had all his old fears resurfacing. Seeing her hold his book in her hands had triggered the past hurt. It was no excuse. He'd blown it. He'd deserved the slap.

Chad lifted his left hand and rubbed his cheek—the sting had dissipated, but the touch of her hand lingered. It had all seemed so clear when he returned from his walk. He was sure Gabby's feelings were as real as his. He had safeguarded his pseudonym for so long and hoped she wouldn't find out who he was until he was positive she was falling for him—Chad, not Brady. Now, he'd killed any chance there might have been between them.

She probably hated his guts and wouldn't speak to him for the rest of his life. He didn't blame her. He hadn't trusted her with the truth. How far could their relationship go without trust?

When Chad woke early the following morning, he wondered why he was in the library sleeping and who had covered him with a blanket. Then he remembered, and he wanted to forget. He'd been such an ass. And all because he'd seen Charles kiss the woman he loved.

Loved? When the hell had that happened?

Chad sat up, rested his elbows on his knees and covered his face with the heel of his hands. He rubbed his eyes, then looked around the room. A soft glow from the window told him it was early morning. It wouldn't be long before everyone would be up and about and ready for breakfast. After last night he didn't think he could face any of them.

Especially Gabby. How could he ever face her again?

The fireplace was cold now, except for a single ember peeking out between the grate full of ashes. It reminded him of himself—his heart was still beating, but something good that had started between him and Gabby had turned to ashes. His fault, of course.

Chad closed his eyes again. A big mistake. He was unable to close his eyes without seeing Gabby—first the shower, the sweetness of her making snow angels, holding Nina in her arms, and tonight, holding her in his arms—rolling on the floor. Her robe had come undone when they had tumbled together. He'd looked down at her. Damn, she was the sexiest lady he'd ever seen. Soft and cuddly in her long teal colored nightshirt that barely covered her thighs. It was nothing like those cold silk negligees of Tanya's he'd never cared for. Sure, they showed a lot of skin, but they weren't something you could snuggle up to on a cold winter's night. And yes, *dammit*, Gabby *had* looked and smelled like a seduction in progress despite what she thought.

She'd looked like a goddess with her long auburn tresses hanging loose around her face. He was certain she'd never worry about messing up a hairdo while making love.

Wow. Stop right there. Do not continue that train of thought.

He threw the blanket aside, stood up, spotting Gabby's soft, over-sized, fluffy slipper socks. Teal, to match her nightshirt. *Hell. When had they slipped off? In the throes of their passionate kiss? When he was as giddy as a schoolboy twirling her around the room before he ruined everything with his vile accusations?*

He picked up the socks, carefully, lovingly, and for the first time in his life wanted to sit back down and cry. Instead, he got up and slowly trudged up to his room, a sock clutched tightly in each hand. He tenderly set them on his dresser. He got undressed and laid on the bed. Maybe when he woke later he'd discover it had all been a bad dream. Maybe then he could live with himself.

Chapter Ten

Chad found his father in the small, informal room off the kitchen later that morning, a steaming cup of coffee in his hands and an empty plate in front of him—the Sunday paper lay spread out on the table.

"Good morning, Son. There's fresh coffee." His dad glanced up from the paper. "You look tired this morning. Had a bad night?"

Ignoring his father, Chad poured a cup of coffee. He needed caffeine in a big way.

"Ethel mentioned seeing you and Gabriella in the library last night." His father folded the paper he'd been reading and tossed it aside, watching Chad settle in the chair opposite him.

Chad frowned at his father, who was calmly adding cream and two heaping teaspoons of sugar to his coffee. He stirred it in quick circular strokes with his spoon as if his life depended on it. Damn. He could tell what was on his father's mind. He took a couple of quick, fortifying gulps of his own steaming cup of caffeine to boost his courage.

"Before you go any further, Dad, I apologize for punching Charles and drawing blood last night in front of company. I don't know what came over me. It doesn't excuse my actions, but I have a feeling there are a lot of men out there who've wanted a piece of him—not to mention he's a nasty drunk. I'm surprised someone hasn't beat me to the punch. Pun intended." He took another deep swig of coffee, and set the cup down. "And you can inform Mother that her matchmaking efforts with Jennifer Newell aren't going to work this time, in case she hasn't figured it out already."

His father didn't bother to hide his knowing grin. "Never underestimate your mother's matchmaking powers, Son. Her track record is undisputed."

Chad made a stab at laughing. "Tell her to stop. I don't need her help."

"It wouldn't do me any good to tell your mother to stop when it comes to matters of the heart. Besides, sometimes we all need a little nudge in the right direction."

"To be honest, I think I blew 'the right direction' part last night."

"Wait a minute." His father put his hands up in front of him, palms outward. He picked up his cup and took a large sip. "I don't think I want to hear about your love life."

"I don't have a love life. That's the point. I am so tired of women wanting me for Bronson B. Brady, I can't see straight. Tanya was the final straw—she took me for a bundle. Now Gabby—well, I just doled out another bundle for Nina in the form of a trust fund and I'm afraid history is about to repeat itself. Love life? Hell, I don't know what to think anymore. Just when I find someone who I think I can give my heart to, I find her with her arms wrapped around one of my books, happier than a Christmas turkey that's been pardoned by the President. What am I to think?"

"To begin with, it's a Thanksgiving turkey not a

Christmas turkey. And I'm sorry about Tanya, Son. I didn't know. But I think what you've done for Nina is commendable regardless of Gabriella's feelings for you, or your feelings for her." Chad's father slid his coffee aside and leaned over the table.

It irked Chad to realize his father didn't even question that he had set up a trust fund for Gabriella's niece.

"Think, Son. Perhaps Gabriella was impressed with your creativity—happy for you, that you're able to give enjoyment to others. You aren't some slob like Charles Denton who lives off his father's name and money. What I think, Son, is you could take a lesson from the President."

"What?" Chad looked at his father, puzzled, the steaming cup halfway to his lips.

"Yep. Sounds to me as if a pardon is in order."

Chad put his cup back on the placemat covered with bright red poinsettias and stared into his coffee cup as if it held the answers to all the secrets of the world. It solved nothing. He was the only one who could make things right.

"Speaking of Charles…"

Chad's head snapped up.

"Charles? Who the hell wants to talk about Charles? I already said I'm sorry."

"Watch your tongue, Son."

"Dad, I'm thirty. I think I can say 'hell.' Hell, my characters in my novels say worse things than that!"

"Yes, but your mother taught you better. Besides you need to learn now so you won't be cussing around your children."

"Children? I don't have any children."

"Yet."

"Jeez, Dad. Did mom put you up to this?" Chad couldn't believe they were having this conversation. His father must have been on leave from work too long, his mother had turned his father's mind to mush. "What is it Mom really wants?

"Leave your mother out of this."

Chad sighed. It was useless. The minute his father uttered the words "leave your mother out of this," the subject was closed for further discussion.

"I want to know why you cold-cocked Charles."

"I'm sorry. I couldn't stand to watch him manhandle Gabby. She doesn't deserve that kind of treatment."

"We had no idea Charles planned to attend, if it makes you feel any better. We wouldn't knowingly put Gabriella in such a position after the horrendous way he's treated her when he found out about Nina. She's been through an awful lot lately, Son. She didn't need another humiliating incident."

Chad didn't think being dumped by Charles was so tragic. Dealing with a baby on one's own, as well as the loss of one's family, however, was probably daunting and stressful. And he'd only added to it.

After last night, he owed her another apology.

****

Gabriella didn't want to leave her bedroom. It was cowardly of her, she knew. She'd never run from anything in her life—always met obstacles head on. But this was different. Facing Chad after slapping his face was not going to be easy.

With the trust fund for Nina, she no longer needed to stay at the Hempstead's. But she wasn't a quitter, either. Tempting as it may be to pack her bags and run, she wasn't about to leave Helen and Chadwick in the lurch. They had been nothing but warm, welcoming, and treated her like one of the family.

She should have trusted her original instincts and refused the position when Chad had shown up accusing her of tracking him down for more money.

She'd overreacted last night. Slapping Chad's face was unforgivable. Letting his kiss go to her head, believing he cared. All right, she had to admit, if only to herself, she was half in love with him. So what? She had thought herself in love with Charles, too, and look where that had gotten her.

Nowhere. Nowhere at all.

Never mind Chad was one of the most handsome men she had ever seen, his relationship with his mother and father was endearing. He really wasn't an uncaring person despite his resistance to marriage and babies. He enjoyed his nieces and nephews and had even been concerned when Nina had cried out. And punching Charles in the nose on her behalf … well, no one had ever done anything so chivalrous on her behalf before. She was so confused she wanted to scream. Instead, she called Mindy, and was relieved when she answered the phone.

"I was hoping you were still in town. Want to go shopping? Today's my day off. We can take Nina and hit the mall and do some Christmas shopping."

"Everything okay? You sound a little upset."

"Just need some time off. Thought we could do lunch. Talk."

"Sure. I'll meet you at the mall center."

"I'll pick you up instead."

With mild temperatures and a blue sky above, Gabriella packed up Nina, the stroller, and left a note with Ethel saying she'd be gone all day. With the holiday season underway, stores opened early and closed late. Gabriella was looking forward to a day of mindless shopping.

Mindy stood in the doorway of the apartment building, a frown on her face. Gabby walked up the path with Nina cuddled over her shoulder.

"Here, let me hold that darling baby." Mindy took her inside and lifted the corner of the blanket. "Look at her smile. What a cutie."

"She's such a good baby, Mindy. I couldn't ask for more. We've bonded. It's as if I'm her real mother now. I love it. It's not so hard once I got used to having her around. Of course, Helen and Ethel have made it easy. They've fallen in love with her, too. Sometimes I can't remember what it was like before Nina."

"But something's wrong," Mindy exclaimed. "So, what's up? You sounded ready to cry when we talked. And you look awful."

"Just what I need to hear. I didn't come here to be insulted," Gabby said. Her attempt at a smile failed.

"Sorry. Sit down. Let's talk."

Mindy carried Nina into the small sitting room, laid her on the couch and unbundled her. She laid the blanket on the floor, and placed Nina in the middle where the infant stretched out kicking and cooing.

"Oh, heavens, will you just look at her," Mindy exclaimed.

"She tries to sit up and wants to stand, now," Gabriella said. "I can't help but think of what my sister is missing. Nina is so like her, it's like looking into her eyes sometimes."

"The family resemblance is strong. She looks like you, too. I can see why someone might mistake her as yours. And that's not a bad thing."

"I wouldn't have it any other way."

"How about a nice cup of hot cider before we go? That'll cheer you up."

Before Gabriella could answer, Mindy jumped up and flew from the room. Within minutes, she was carrying two mugs of steaming cider from the kitchen, the spicy aroma of cinnamon followed her into the small room. She handed a cup to Gabby, and sat down.

"Okay, girlfriend. I can see something else has upset you, and it doesn't have anything to do with Nina. I've never seen you look this upset. I know your life has been a roller coaster lately. But you've handled it better than I would have. So, what's been going on?"

Gabriella looked at her friend, tears filling her eyes. Mindy was right. Her life was a roller coaster and she'd been too busy to mourn the loss of her family. The pain was still there—she'd simply tucked it aside in order to get through each day.

When she didn't respond right away, Mindy jumped to her own conclusions, concern written all over her face.

"Oh, my God. It's Charles, isn't it? That...that..." Mindy looked at Nina before whispering across the blanket. "That b-a-s-t-a-r-d!"

Gabriella laughed. "You don't have to spell it out. Nina isn't old enough to understand what you're saying. But you're right. It is about Charles. He showed up at the Hempstead's with Jennifer Newell for a holiday gathering last night."

Lord, was it only last night? It seemed like months ago.

Gabriella smiled at the comical expression on Mindy's face.

"You were right the first time. I don't know what I ever saw in him. Why I stayed with him for so long. I guess I was so focused on my career that our cool relationship, for lack of a better word, seemed to fit."

"So, what'd he do now?"

"He kissed me under the mistletoe in front of everyone—thought he could rekindle something we didn't have in the first place. He said some nasty things to me. That's when Chad punched him in the nose."

"Chad punched Charles in the nose?" Mindy gasped, then broke out laughing. "I wish I'd been there to see that. Chad's my hero."

"Well, it wasn't funny at the time. Charles was a bit tipsy."

"You mean drunk?"

"Yes. He was furious. You should have seen his face, besides the blood, I mean. He was not a happy camper."

"Blood? Chad drew blood? Oh, my. Chad must have the hots for you."

"I was beginning to think so, too, until later that night. I inadvertently found out he's a famous author. He accused me of knowing all along—that I was only after him because of his money."

"Famous author?" Mindy couldn't hide her curiosity.

Gabriella proceeded to tell Mindy about the incident, including the part about Chad's kiss.

"He was very insulting, so I slapped his face and

walked out. Now I feel guilty. I haven't seen him today, and I'm sure he never wants to see me again, either."

"If you need a place to stay, you can move back in here with me. Trish left in a hurry. No idea what's going on—you know Trish, she keeps to herself most of the time. She packed her bags, left a note on the table and took off two days ago. Paid her share of the rent through January, and hopped a plane to France."

"France? What's in France?"

"I think her mother lives there. Trish doesn't talk about her much, since her parents divorced a year ago. Anyway, it'd be just you, me, and Nina."

"It's very enticing. And believe me, I've considered leaving, especially since I don't need the job any longer. But, I can't leave Helen—she's been like a mother to me and a grandmother to Nina. Even Ethel is a darling."

"So, what are you going to do?"

"Nothing right now. When I'm ready, Dennis offered to help me move after the holidays."

"Dennis? Does he visit the Hempsteads often?"

"He's been there a couple of times. Actually he was there last night and ended up taking Jennifer home."

Mindy started paying a lot of attention to Nina.

"Mindy, Mindy, Mindy. I think you have the hots for Dennis."

"I do not."

"Do too. It's written all over your face even though you're trying not to let it show. You only met Dennis once."

"Twice."

"Twice?"

Her friend was embarrassed. She'd admitted as much—she hoped Mindy wasn't putting too much stock in the Hempstead's CEO.

"You mistakenly assumed you were in love with Andy and that he cared for you. Don't make the same mistake with Dennis. I know I've learned my lesson. Not once, but twice."

"You've fallen for Chad, haven't you?" Mindy asked, a broad smile on her face, taking the pressure off herself. "I knew it."

"I thought Chad was starting to care for me until he turned into this big Jekyll/Hyde person. Lord, Mindy, he's a famous author. I found a whole series of his books in his parents' library. I was going to read one when he interrupted me, and that's when the whole thing took a turn for the worst, and I slapped his face."

"Oh, my. Did you slap Charles' face when he kissed you and created a scene?"

"No. No, I didn't."

"Hmmm. I wonder why? Could it be you really didn't care that Charles hurt you, but cared that Chad did? Sounds to me as if Chad has gotten under your skin."

Gabriella stood up. "I think it's time to go shopping."

"Good idea. We can go to the bookstore and see what your famous author has out there in print. Does he write under his own name?"

"No. At least I'm not sure if he does. I only know about the ones by Bronson B. Brady—a crime detective kind of novel."

"Bronson B. Brady? Oh! My! God! Bronson B. Brady is famous! I love his books. They're terrific.

Let's go do some detective work of our own."

Gabriella thoroughly enjoyed her afternoon shopping trip with Mindy. It was just what she needed to get her mind off everything, although the memory of Chad's kiss still lingered.

She decided to have Nina's picture taken on Santa's lap. After all, a baby's first Christmas only happened once in a lifetime. Gabriella wanted to make sure she'd have pictures and memories for when Nina was grown. Gabriella vowed she would do everything in her power to see Nina had a wonderful childhood regardless of how hard she had to work, or the sacrifices she'd have to endure to make it happen. It would all be worth it.

Christmas greens and red bows hung from the ceiling and posts in the center of the mall. Dressed in black pants, white shirts, red jackets, and elfin green hats, the local community chorus sang one Christmas song after another, presenting a very festive atmosphere. A large tree shaped out of hundreds of poinsettias stood behind Santa's North Pole. It was a heart-warming and comforting scene, and Gabriella thrilled at the sight. Even Nina was fascinated by it all.

Picture taken, Nina tucked snugly into the stroller once again, Gabriella and Mindy finished their shopping. The mall's walkways were full of individual crafters and specialty shops for the season, making it easy to find a little something for each of the Hempsteads and Chad's nieces and nephews. She found a snow angel tree ornament, a reminder of her frolic in the snow with Chad. In spite of their argument last night, she couldn't resist purchasing it.

Finally, exhausted and hungry, they stayed at the

mall for dinner. Once seated, Gabriella asked the waitress to warm Nina's bottle, and while they waited for their meal to arrive, Gabriella held Nina on her lap and fed her. Nina feasted greedily on the warm milk, while tiny fingers grasped the bottle to keep it in place.

"You look so natural holding her," Mindy said. "I think you were meant to be a mom. Someday maybe you'll have one of your own."

"I'd like that—a brother or sister for Nina." Gabriella pictured a little boy who looked an awful lot like Chad.

Get a grip. It is not going to happen. Not after last night.

"What about you?" Gabriella turned the tables on Mindy. "You're wonderful with Nina. You'd make a great mom, too."

"Do you really think so?"

"Definitely."

Their dinner arrived and any words of wisdom died on Gabriella's lips as Nina gave a hearty burp, a reaction to being patted softly on her back. Unfortunately along with the burp, Nina spit up, staining Gabriella's sweater. With quick reflexes, Gabriella whisked them both to the lady's room where she washed Nina and herself, and changed Nina's diaper before returning to their table. Gabriella placed Nina back in the stroller where she began kicking her chubby legs and arms and making gurgling sounds at the same time. Gabriella made sure Nina was secure before finally getting a chance to finish eating her own meal.

"So much for motherhood," Mindy said, chuckling.

"It's worth it, Mindy. I'm learning to take it all in

stride, just like everything else."

"Speaking of men, we haven't checked out the bookstore yet."

"Who said anything about men?" Gabriella smiled.

"We were about to and you know it. What say we go to the bookstore after we eat? Nina's been so good, and she's just about asleep. She'll survive another hour at the mall."

Gabby hesitated. Mindy continued.

"Don't worry, we'll have you sneaking back in the Hempstead's so you can escape running into Chad before he even knows you've been gone."

"I really need to apologize—the sooner the better. But it doesn't have to be today."

When they arrived at the bookstore, they were surprised to see two rows of books with Bronson B. Brady's name on the spine. A stirring of pride washed over her. She picked out one and read the back cover, then studied the embossed front cover with his name in big letters across the top.

"Here, you'll love this one. It's one of the Dean Reynolds Detective series you mentioned," Mindy said, handing her a book.

Gabriella looked at it: *Award Winner. New York Times' #1 Best Seller.* She ran her hand over the cover and carefully turned the pages and began reading. She was intrigued. Instead of being caught trying to borrow one from the Hempstead's library, Gabriella decided to purchase Chad's latest release. She wanted to find out just how talented *Bronson B. Brady* was. Maybe reading his books would give her some insight into the complex man.

"Let me buy it," Mindy grabbed the book away

from her.

"You don't have to do that. I can afford a book."

"That's not the point. I'll let you read it if you agree to get Bronson B. Brady to autograph it for me."

"I think you'd have a better chance of getting his autograph than I would at the moment. He'll probably throw the book back at me."

****

A constant procession of visitors stopped by the Hempstead's laden with Christmas baskets full of an assortment of homemade baked goods to wish his mother well and spread holiday cheer. With all the festive food coming into the house, Chad figured Ethel wouldn't have to bake anything until next July. Ethel set out for one group of visitors what the previous visitors had brought. This continued on and off all day until well into the evening. Chad gave up waiting for Gabby to come home. Instead, he retreated to his room wondering where she'd been all day—was she coming back at all?

He took a deep breath, sat down at his computer, and turned it on. Dean Reynolds might just as well get lucky with the ladies tonight and have a hot night out on the old town tonight on Chad's behalf, because he sure as hell wasn't going to.

By the time Dean picked up his date, had dinner, took the lady home with an invitation to stay for breakfast, not to mention one long, hot steamy shower shared in one tight shower stall and a sultry, sexy, satisfyingly long, long night having hot, slow, slow, sometimes fast sex, Chad was exhausted. And so hot, so hard, and so ready to head for a cold shower himself, he was tempted to by-pass the washroom down the hall and go right to Gabriella's room and beg forgiveness. As well as ask other favors.

Chad wanted Gabriella. It was all Dean's fault—Dean had gotten what Chad wanted.

Dean Reynolds was one happy man tonight. After his night of lovemaking, he'd gone on to solve his case, win the police detective department's highest award for his efforts and bravery, and then flew off into the sunset with his lady-love at his side to a remote part of the world while he waited for the next crime case to come along.

Chad's own love life was just about as boring as a dead rat's. Reflecting back was painful. He meant it when he told his father he was tired of women chasing after him for financial gain and security. But he was wrong about Gabby.

He rubbed his cheek. He'd deserved her slap.

At two in the morning, Chad was still lying on top of the covers, his mind wandering in circles trying to figure it all out. Gabby wasn't like those other women. His father was right. He had to apologize, had to ask Gabby for a pardon—even if it didn't change things between them. It was the right thing to do.

In the meantime, a cold shower might cool him down enough so he could get his mind off her and get some sleep.

Chapter Eleven

Arriving back at the Hempstead's, Gabriella entered the library to let Helen know she was home.

"I'm glad you had a lovely time, dear. You look tired. Off to bed with you and Nina. I'll see you in the morning. We can have a nice chat after church services tomorrow over tea, and you can tell me all about your day."

Grateful Helen wasn't in the mood to chat, Gabriella carried Nina and her shopping bag up to their room. She treaded quietly up the stairs and down the hallway, hoping Chad was engrossed in his writing and wouldn't hear her footsteps. Gently closing her bedroom door, she settled Nina for the night and climbed in bed with one of the books she'd let Mindy buy. Before she knew it, her bedside digital clock flashed two o'clock in the morning. The book had indeed held her interest. She didn't want to put it down. But she had to get some sleep soon, otherwise she would have a hard time keeping up with Nina and Helen's schedule in the morning. Deciding a quick shower would relax her tight muscles so she could get a good night's sleep, Gabriella checked on Nina, gathered her toiletries and padded down the hall to the washroom.

Adjusting the water, she drew the shower curtain around the tub and proceeded to undress, laying her clothes carefully to the side. Stepping into the tub, Gabriella changed the knobs on the faucet, allowing the hot water to fill up around her.

She stood up to reach for the bottle of bath foam from above the sink. The door swung open. Chad stood frozen in place in a pair of tight, white briefs—his only clothing. His hair tousled, his eyes glazed, his body…all too intriguing… and sexy as hell.

Gabriella gasped. She tucked the shower curtain around her, but it clung to her wet skin.

Chad's mouth dropped open, then shut.

"So, we meet again," he said, his eyebrows raised, his hands resting on his hips.

Gabby took a deep breath to calm her racing heart.

"I can see you haven't learned to knock."

"Sorry, I didn't see a sticky note on the door. Didn't realize anyone was still up, otherwise I would've put my pants on. I didn't hear the shower running. Sorry."

Neither moved.

Gabriella's gaze was drawn to his tight abs, his muscular thighs, and all his other magnificent body parts straining against his briefs.

"Do I pass inspection?" His voice was low, sexual, and barely audible.

Startled by his boldness, Gabriella gasped. His half grin and cocky stance unnerved her. His words shocked her back to her own predicament—her nude state and his near-nude body together in the same room. Standing, admiring each other had disaster written all over it. She sank down into the tub—there were no bubbles to hide her body parts, and the heat now circling throughout her body had nothing to do with the hot water in the tub.

"Do you mind?" she demanded behind the shower curtain.

"Nope."

Oh, Lord. Gabriella wanted him to go away. She wanted him to disappear. She wanted him to... *Dammit.* She wanted him. She had never wanted anyone as much as she wanted Chad Hempstead.

Gabriella held her breath and waited. It was too quiet in the room. Slowly, she peeled back the shower curtain and peeked around it. He hadn't moved an inch. She dropped the curtain back in place and prayed he'd disappear. When that didn't work, she counted to ten. Slowly.

"Go away," she demanded.

"No."

Damn. Now what?

"Please. Just go away so I can get out."

"You just got in."

"Go away."

"What do you need?"

Gabriella sighed. Perhaps if she told him, he'd get it and leave.

"Bubble bath. Now go away."

The shower curtain moved. A muscular, hairy arm appeared, holding a cream-colored bottle of bath foam over her head.

"Thanks."

"Don't mention it."

He was still in the room, she could sense him, feel his presence with every cell of her being. She wanted to cry out in frustration, in embarrassment, and just because. She was tired from shopping, she was tired of sparing with him, and tired of having to deal with the hand fate had dealt her.

Gabriella poured a hearty dollop of liquid from the bottle into the bath water and splashed it around until bubbles formed along the top of the water. He could stand there all night if he wanted. She didn't care. She wasn't getting out.

She slid down into the deep tub, rested her head along the edge, and closed her eyes. And hiccupped!

"Are you all right?"

She wrung out the washcloth and placed it over her face.

"Fine," she hiccupped again, wishing him away.

"You don't sound fine. Are you crying?"

"I never cry."

"It sounds like you're crying."

"Go away." She hiccupped once more. "I'm fine."

"Listen, Gabby, I'm really sorry about last night. I didn't mean to hurt you. I've felt like a heel ever since I kissed you."

Gabriella sat up in the tub. Water sloshed over the rim. *He was sorry he'd kissed her? It had been a wonderful kiss—she couldn't stop thinking about it.* Obviously their kiss didn't matter to him if he was sorry he kissed her. On top of everything else, if that didn't put her in her place, nothing did.

"I'm sorry, too. I'm sorry I slapped you. You hurt my feelings, but that was no excuse."

"I understand. But you didn't slap Charles' face. Why is that?"

"You didn't give me a chance," she said, suddenly realizing the truth of it. "You slugged him before I had a chance."

"I wonder why?"

His voice low, Gabriella almost missed his words. Mortified at his comments and their entire conversation, Gabriella slipped deeper into the tub and immersed her entire body underwater, head included, hoping he would just go away so she could be humiliated all on her own.

But her respite from his closeness was short lived. Two hands lifted her from the tub and the now cool water without ceremony, and she was held tightly against one strong, warm, firm, enticing unclothed body—skin to skin.

"What do you think you're doing?" Chad whispered harshly against her ear as his face found the curve of her neck. He put her down on the melon-colored throw rug, not letting her go. "Were you trying to drown yourself? God, woman, you scared the hell out of me."

Spitting and sputtering, Gabriella's hair clung to her head, neck, and shoulders, while bubbles slid slowly down her back. Her skin, slick and silky from the foam, was definitely aware of his warm, firm, solid body. He held her tight against him in a sensual embrace. Clasped so close and so tenderly, his reaction to their contact was evident. Her breasts were held captive against a very warm chest, as bubbles continued to slither down her skin in a slow, erotic path. His lips found hers and Gabriella floated, adrift at sea.

His hardness nestled against her, leaving little doubt as to his own desires. Belatedly, Gabriella extricated herself from his side, for it was sheer madness the reaction he was causing. She shivered, hot and dizzy all at the same time.

"No-no-" she stuttered, not knowing whether it was in answer to his question, or to try to stop herself from letting her emotions run riot.

His arms gripped her tighter. She was about to die from the pleasure of it. Her arms slid up and circled his neck at the same time his lips covered hers in another deep, penetrating kiss. As if aware her knees were about to give out, Chad lifted her off the floor and cradled her in his arms.

"I'm so, so sorry, Gabby. I didn't mean to hurt you last night."

"If you apologize for kissing me one more time, I'll scream," she murmured against his lips.

"Apologize? For kissing you?" he asked. "You've got it all wrong. No, Sweetheart, I was apologizing for what happened after the kiss. I never apologize for kissing a lady. Especially one as enticing as you. It's all I think about anymore—kissing you. Well, that and other things..."

Gabriella remembered they were still naked, far more than just toe-to-toe. Shyness washed over her, she snuggled into his neck.

Chad set her feet back on the rug, lifted her chin and looked deep into her eyes. He slowly wrapped a bath towel around her shivering body, her arms still around his neck.

"This goes against every principle I've ever had when I have a beautiful, enticing and naked woman in my arms—letting her go when I have her just where I want her—in my arms."

"What if she doesn't want to be let go?" It was a softly stated question she shouldn't have asked. She grabbed at the towel like a lifeline and stepped back from his embrace.

Chad took a deep breath and let it out slowly.

"I don't think we're ready for this yet. There's still too much unsettled between us that might get in the way."

Chad made a pretense of making sure the large, fluffy towel was securely in place before ushering her out of the washroom and down the hall to her room.

"What are you doing?" she asked.

"Obviously, being a gentleman—and a fool," he said, chuckling. "With you wrapped around me, naked, it's becoming impossible. It's late and I'm sure Nina isn't going to let you sleep in. I'll see you in the morning. We'll talk."

Gabriella gazed into his handsome face, and smiled. She must be crazy. She wasn't sure where this latest episode was taking her, but right now she didn't care. Chad had kissed her again, and it was even better than the last time. He didn't believe she was after his fortune. This time she truly believed he trusted her.

He leaned down and placed a quick but firm kiss on her willing lips, turned and retreated down the hall. He took his time, his white briefs hugging his muscular backside. He turned and caught her staring. Gabriella smiled back. He winked. Her heart sang.

Oh, Lord. What just happened?

Gabriella shook her head. If he hadn't pulled the plug on her feelings they would have made love.

She lay down on the queen-sized bed, sinking into the old-fashioned feather tick coverlet. Gabriella closed her eyes and wondered what it would be like to make love with Chad. Chad didn't think she was ready, but she was never more ready in her entire life than she was at this moment. The feelings that coursed through her body when he touched her were like none she'd ever known. She tingled, came alive, responded to him, his kisses, the touch of his skin against hers. The feel of his hardness against her turned her blood to molten lava. Just thinking about it made her mouth go dry as the heat from her body burned at the inner core of her being. It was amazing. It was all consuming.

Gabriella opened her eyes, turned toward the window and gazed out at the soft, lazy snowflakes drifting past the window in the moonlight. Nina turned over in her crib and sighed. With an effort, Gabriella got out of bed, the towel slipping to the floor. Instead of picking it up and re-wrapping it around her still damp body, she slipped into her nightshirt, and wrapped her hair turban style with the towel. She padded across the floor to check on Nina.

The room was warm, and the blanket-sleeper Nina wore was sufficient to keep her snugly all night long, but Gabriella made sure all was well.

She leaned down to kiss the sleeping baby—a precious miracle.

Chad was right. They had a lot to settle between them before a lasting relationship could form. In her heart, she wanted more than a one-night stand. But was he ready for a long-term relationship?

The following morning, with Nina bathed and fed, she dallied hoping to avoid Chad—hoping he'd already been down for breakfast and gone back to his room to work so she wouldn't have to face him right away. She had doubts about last night. Her feelings still raw, she wasn't quite sure what his feelings were toward her. Sure, there was chemistry between them, but was it enough for a lasting relationship? She wasn't about to lay her heart bare if he didn't love her in return. If he didn't trust her with who he was—a famous writer. Would he accept Nina as part of her life, or would he consider her nothing but a distraction? What about her degree? Although her encounter with Chad the night before was explosive, and opened new doors for both of them, she needed to be cautious with her heart.

There were too many questions to be answered.

Gabriella's spirits fell when Helen told her Chad was called back to Manhattan and had already left.

"He should be home on Wednesday," Helen said.

"Did he finish his novel?" Gabriella asked, excited, but inwardly upset he never mentioned that he was going back to the city last night. *Not even a goodbye, I'll see you Wednesday.*

More doubts niggled.

Ethel and Helen looked at each other, then at Gabriella.

"Yes, I know about his books," Gabriella said, smiling at their puzzled looks. "I found out quite by accident." She didn't explain.

Ethel's expression changed, the smile indicating perhaps she knew something.

"My, my," Helen said, lifting Nina against her shoulder to make the baby more comfortable. "How did my son react when he found out you knew about his writing?"

"Not well, I must say. He was very upset."

"It's nothing personal, you know," Helen said, patting Nina on the back in a slow rhythmic motion. "It's a closely guarded secret. He tries not to let people know about his career until he gets to know them better."

"Why ever not? I read one of his books last night and it's very good."

"It's the women, you see. Once they find out who he really is, they go after him because of his fame and fortune. He's become very jaded, I'm afraid."

"Oh," Gabriella exclaimed. Helen's concern and love for her son was clear. She understood now why he was so protective, and why he didn't trust her when he'd found his book in her hand. It all made perfect sense. But it didn't explain Chad's reaction to her when he lifted her from the tub and held her close. Was he beginning to care? To trust her?

Ethel poured tea. Several minutes later, Sheila and her kids stopped by for a visit.

"We're all going caroling next Saturday evening. Why don't you join us, Gabby? There'll be about thirty of us and we usually have a ball—kids and all!"

"It sounds lovely, but I'd rather not take Nina out in the evening air. It's too cold to take her out in a stroller."

"Now, dear, Nina is still young enough to be no problem for me and Ethel. You can feed her before you go, and we'll keep her here and rock her by the fire and enjoy ourselves 'til you all return. Devon, too," Helen turned to Sheila. "I hope you'll let him stay with us, as well."

"Thanks, Mom. We won't be gone long, and he's still too little to do anything but sleep."

"He can sleep on my lap." Helen smiled. "Now with all that settled, I need you ladies to do some shopping for me seeing as I can't get around very well in this contraption."

"We can take you to the mall and wheel you wherever you want to go. It shouldn't be too crowded this afternoon."

"No, no. Perhaps if the weather was. better. Besides, I'd rather stay with Ethel and enjoy the children. You girls go and have a good time."

"Give us a list and we'll tackle it for you," Sheila said. "How about it, Gabby, want to come along? The men plan to watch the kids so we can have a mom's day out. Jodi is going to join us, too."

"I'll call Mindy to see if she'll keep Nina for a couple of hours."

"My dear, Nina can stay here."

"Helen, you're too kind, but as you're going to watch her while I go caroling, I'm sure Mindy won't mind in the least. I'll give her a call right now."

But Mindy was busy, much to Gabriella's surprise, apparently a dinner date. Ethel and Helen kept Nina after all.

****

Gabriella was still in bed when Chad left Monday morning—he hadn't wanted to wake her. Overwhelmed by holding her naked body in his arms the night before, he'd forgotten all about the call from his agent wanting to meet with him on Monday. He figured he'd be back no later than Wednesday morning. He and Gabby could talk and work everything out between them. His meager apology didn't explain his behavior near enough. He had so much more he wanted to say to her, but being so close to her, touching her, breathing in her scent, had taken away all his coherent thoughts.

He arrived in Manhattan only to discover major changes were needed on his latest manuscript, and his agent had arranged meetings with the editor, not to mention a last minute release book signing scheduled for Friday.

On Tuesday evening while attending the publisher's evening social, Tanya, his ex-fiancée, tapped him on the shoulder.

"Long time, no see, Bronson, Baby." Her deep shimmering pink painted lips smiled and pouted at the same time.

How had he ever considered those lips enticing?

"The name is Chad, as in Chadwick Hempstead," he said.

"I know, darling. But you *are* Bronson B. Brady, and I've always found that charming."

"You found my money charming. Whose shirttail have you got a hold of this time? Don't tell me you're here alone? Maureen wouldn't knowingly have invited you to this affair otherwise." Chad retrieved a drink from one of the many trays being passed around. He desperately needed something to calm his nerves.

"You haven't changed, Bron Baby. You're still the old stuffy bore you always were. I can't understand how you can write such exciting sexy detective books and be so unemotional in real life."

"You never complained when we were together, if I remember correctly."

Tanya tucked her arm through Chad's and nudged closer, her breasts rubbed against his arm through her flimsy dress, the cleavage dipping down to her navel.

Chad looked into her eyes, raised his eyebrows, and shook his head. He disentangled her from his side just as Ned Harper, another author, approached.

"Darling, you didn't tell me you knew Chadwick.

How interesting. Chadwick, how've you been?" Ned offered his hand and Chad took it in a firm grip. "My congratulations on your new release. I envy you—you've had a long run."

"I hear you're not doing too shabby yourself—another three-book contract following your last Sci-fi trilogy. Not bad."

Tanya smiled up at Ned, her slender fingers and long cherry talons now wrapped around the other author's arm. Obviously Ned was enamored with her, too. Chad felt sorry for Ned. On the other hand, Chad was relieved he'd escaped Tanya's clutches, no matter the cost.

Seeing Tanya again had all the old emotional baggage and doubts about whether Gabby cared for him or for Brady crowded his mind. After all, it was only *after* she'd discovered his pseudonym that she seemed to truly want him, wasn't it?

Tanya led Ned across the room. She turned and smiled. A very satisfied smile.

He'd never considered himself stuffy, and it bothered him to think Tanya thought of him that way. Did others? Did his family think he was stuffy, too? From the way Gabby responded to him, he didn't think she thought he was stuffy at all. Unless it was all an act.

Damn Tanya for putting doubts in his mind.

Chad lifted his almost full glass of champagne to his taut lips and drank heartily. He didn't think he was stuffy. He had made snow angels. He'd taken part in a wild snowball fight. He'd decorated a Christmas tree. And he'd had a blast. He was truly alive for the first time in years. His sisters and their families weren't so bad after all. Gabby as well as her baby had tugged on his heartstrings—holding Nina had been an emotional experience. He wondered what it would be like to have a baby of his own. He'd never wanted children, but after the last few weeks at home with Gabby, he began to change his mind.

About a lot of things.

Chad scanned the crowded, noisy room. It wasn't where he wanted to be. He put his glass down, made his excuses to his host, and left. It was almost three in the morning when he found his way back to his empty studio in mid-Manhattan.

Alone in his cold, dark, spotless apartment, Chad realized his life was incomplete. And lonely. He wondered if Gabby was thinking about him. He wanted to call her but wasn't sure what to say. They had left so much unsaid. He couldn't forget how she had responded to him. She had been too willing—much too willing. He had been the one to put a stop to their last encounter. Gabby had looked disappointed. Now, he wasn't sure how genuine her feelings really were. Meeting up with Tanya again did nothing but skew his perspective on his and Gabby's relationship.

As the hectic week continued, Chad found it harder and harder to pick up the phone and call home. On Thursday morning, his mother called to see if he was coming home for Christmas.

"Yes. I'm almost done with the changes and negotiations. I have a book-signing on Friday evening for the Christmas rush. I plan to drive home afterwards," Chad promised. He was ready to leave the city behind.

"After having you home the last couple of weeks, it would be a disappointment if you didn't make it back for Christmas Eve," Chad's mother sighed. "Everyone is caroling Saturday evening."

"I'm not sure I'll make it for the caroling, but I'll be home for Christmas."

Silence.

"So, how's Dad? Has he been going to the office all week?"

"He's fine. Yes, he feels better knowing I'm not alone all day."

Silence.

"How's Ethel? Still baking up a storm?"

"Son. I know you don't give a fig about Ethel's baking. Why don't you get right to the point? Why don't you ask me about Gabriella?"

"Is she still there?"

"Still here? Yes she's still here. Why would she leave?"

"No reason, I guess."

"What's been going on, Chad? She's wearing one of the longest faces I've ever seen. What have you done now?"

"Mother…"

"Don't 'mother' me. I'm not blind. The two of you have been dancing around each other since you both got here. Why don't you just admit you're attracted to her? You haven't met up with Tanya again, have you? That woman is an evil witch."

"Mother…"

"Junior?"

"Listen, I've got to go or I'll be late for my meeting."

"I wasn't just trying to goad you when I said Gabriella was too good for you, you know. I think the two of you are perfect for each other."

"Mother, I do have a meeting and if I don't leave now they'll probably cancel my contract."

"Not likely. You bring in too much revenue for them. Just talk to her. Give her a chance."

"I'll see you this weekend," Chad said, ringing off.

He should've known he couldn't keep anything from his mother. Her matchmaking skills *were* undisputable!

****

By Friday night Chad still hadn't appeared. It was as if he were a figment of her imagination. Except his books were real, and his picture on the back cover was real. She stared at it every night—had it memorized, waiting for him to walk through the door to tell her what happened between them was real, and that he missed her. That he loved her as she loved him. But there had been too much left unsaid between them. And he'd been gone all week without so much as a word. She didn't know what to expect.

Lord, what had she been reduced to? A couple of kisses—a couple of very toe-curling kisses—had literally knocked her socks off. Which reminded her, she still hadn't found her slipper-socks. Ethel must have picked them up and put them in the laundry. She would have to ask about them later.

By Saturday afternoon, Gabriella had worked herself into a tizzy. She'd overheard Helen on the phone talking to Chad, and she could only assume they'd been discussing her still being at the Hempstead's. Had Chad expected her to pack up and leave? Had he changed his mind and didn't have feelings for her after all? Was he staying in New York?

Had she been a fool to fall in love with a man who was just using her?

And who the hell was Tanya?

Heart heavy, she really didn't have the spirit to go caroling with the others. It had been a long week, and the closer it got to Christmas, the more she missed her own family. Even though she wasn't up to socializing, she had to admit it would help lift her spirits to get out and enjoy herself.

Dressing in black wool slacks, a red ribbed turtleneck sweater, and a pair of black insulated, ankle-high boots, Gabriella put on her coat and gloves and headed toward the staircase to go down and join Jodi and the others. When she reached the top of the stairs, she met Chad racing up the stairs. He took them two at a time, his jacket unzipped, hanging open, gloves in hand. His hair was windblown. He was the most devastatingly handsome man she'd ever seen. Her heart stopped, jump started, and kicked into overdrive.

He looked up at her. Her smile froze. He didn't return her smile. What had she done, now?

"Hello. How was New York?" she asked softly—politely. She wanted him to take her in his arms and kiss her. She had missed him. Missed his kisses. Each night she'd closed her eyes and envisioned them making love. From the look on his face, he didn't reciprocate those feelings.

Gabriella swallowed and tucked her hands in her pockets. "Excuse me. Jodi and Sheila are waiting downstairs. We're about to go caroling."

"I know. The kids are excited, too," he said.

It was as if they had never kissed, as if he had never held her naked body in his arms.

"New York was busy. I was busy," he said, as if it explained everything.

"Yes. Your mother told me."

She sidestepped him to go down the stairs—her heart pounded in her ears. She trembled, upset at his demeanor, and hoped she wouldn't fall on her way down. "I have to go."

"I'm going, too."

Her head snapped up. He had just returned from the city. Had he only come back to pack up his belongings and head back to New York? She couldn't breathe. Was he going back to this Tanya woman?

"Go?" she whispered, her voice cracking.

"Yes, I'm going, too. I'm caroling with the family."

"Oh." It came out in a slow whoosh. "Oh."

Gabriella didn't know whether she was glad he was staying, or upset at the way he was behaving. He stood still, watching her, giving nothing away. What could she say? Do?

She hid the hurt, and turned away.

"Tell them I'll be down in a minute," he said to her retreating back.

He shut his bedroom door, leaving her to her own miserable thoughts.

Five minutes later he joined everyone in the hallway where they were discussing car-pooling.

"You and Chad can ride with us," Sheila said. "We have a new seven-person van. It's our Christmas present to ourselves. We need it with our big family. So, seeing as Devon's staying here, there's plenty of room without the car seat in the back. Don't know why we didn't buy a van sooner."

She laughed along with the others gathered in the foyer.

At least Gabriella didn't have to ride alone with Chad in his vehicle. The way he was acting, she knew he was going to tell her it had all been a big mistake and it was over between them before it even got started. She'd anticipated this all week, and now his actions said it all.

Chapter Twelve

The community center was abuzz with more than two dozen carolers waiting to get started. Hot cider and cocoa were already available next to a table piled high with an assortment of cookies. Chad followed his family into the room, surprised to see Dennis, cup in hand, next to a woman he didn't know. Gabby stepped forward, arms outstretched and hurried toward the couple. Chad frowned at her enthusiasm for his friend.

"Mindy. You rascal. Don't tell me your dinner date the other night was with Dennis?" Gabby said.

The two women hugged. Confused, Chad's eyebrows rose in a silent question to his friend.

"Hi, Gabby. It's good to see you," Dennis said. He wrapped his arms around her shoulders and gave her a hug. "Did you get all those papers signed for Nina's trust fund?"

"Yes. But how did you know?"

Dennis' eyebrows raised, he looked around sheepishly, then looked down at his feet. Chad was about to drag him outside and give his friend a good talking to.

"Uh, Chad...I...ah... I ..."

"I guess I must have mentioned it over dinner the other night," Mindy said. "I didn't think you'd mind."

Mindy's face turned an embarrassing shade of pale. *Just what was going on?*

"You remember Mindy, Gabriella's roommate? Mindy this is Chad Hempstead," Dennis said.

"I know. The famous author," Mindy beamed, extending her hand. "I bought several of your books. They're great. Would you autograph one for me sometime?"

Chad looked from Mindy to Gabriella and frowned.

"Glad to meet you. Bring your books around sometime and I'd be happy to autograph them for you."

As the evening got underway, Gabriella joined his sister and nieces, leaving him behind. He smiled, observing her interactions with his family—holding his nieces' hands as they walked down streets lined with homes bedecked with colored lights and festive greens for the season. He couldn't take his eyes off her as she sang songs, smiled at those who opened their doors to listen to the spirit of Christmas. He was awed by her serenity.

He suddenly didn't care whether she wanted him or Bronson B. Brady. They were one and the same, and they both wanted her.

He worked his way toward her, but his nieces surrounded her, with Constance winning the handholding contest for the evening. If he didn't know any better, he'd think Gabby was avoiding him.

He couldn't get the feel of her soft skin against his naked body out of his mind. She was a desirable woman. He wanted to get close to her again. Now.

The caroling dragged on forever. Although Chad enjoyed singing at the nursing home and the children's center, he felt like an outsider. His sisters, and Dennis and Mindy were being over-protective of Gabby. He desperately wanted to be a part of their inner circle. But every time he worked his way up to her side, one of them appeared to catch her attention. Or someone he hadn't seen in a while would monopolize his time.

When he finally got close to her, Dennis nudged him aside.

"Get all those books signed in New York?" his friend asked, a wicked grin on his face.

"Yeah, about a hundred of them." Chad couldn't hide his annoyance and gritted his teeth. "What about you? Contracts going well at the office?" Not expecting an answer, Chad turned to speak to Gabby. But she had drifted to the other side of the room, his sisters on either side of her.

Damn!

On the way home, Chad found himself relegated to the back seat. Once again Gabby sat in the middle with Constance resting her tiny, tired head on Gabby's shoulder—Gabby's arm snuggling her as tight as the seatbelts would allow.

Chad groaned. Once they got back home, he was determined to get Gabby alone so they could talk and finally get things out in the open. They rode through the city streets where holiday lights sparkled in the night, but Chad was oblivious, his mind only on Gabby.

Once home, Chad's mother invited everyone to stay for hot cocoa. To entice everyone, Ethel wheeled out a tray overflowing with her latest batch of cookies straight from the oven.

"My, my, look at all of you," Helen called when they'd assembled in the library. "My family. Now come on over here by the fire and tell me all about your evening. Did you have a good time?"

"We visited sick people and people who don't have homes," Constance ran up to her grandmother, receiving a warm hug and a kiss on the cheek. "Sara and 'Anna memorized all the words to the songs, but I didn't. Gabby helped me. She's nice. I like her best."

"We all do, dear. Now why don't you go help yourself to some of those cookies Ethel just set out over there."

Kids—they were a handful. Just being around his family the past few weeks had been an eye-opener. They were pretty neat, and a lot of fun, too.

"Chad, come wheel this contraption over to the piano so I can play a few Christmas tunes. Come on, everyone, time to join in before you all go home."

As requested, they all gathered in a semi-circle around the piano to sing Christmas Carols while his mother played. Sheila held Devon, cradling him in her arms. Chad looked over at Gabby holding Nina in the same warm, motherly fashion. Emotions welled up in his chest. He couldn't breathe. He pictured her with another child snuggled close against her breast—his child. He swallowed. Hard. He was unable to sing a single note.

He worked his way over to her side and stood behind her, breathing in her scent—the fresh outdoors mingled in her hair, her clothes, along with a faint hint of baby powder and lotion. It was the most erotic fragrance he'd ever smelled. He didn't say a word, or even touch her. He couldn't believe how aware he was of her.

He couldn't wait for everyone to leave so he could get her alone. Make love to her.

He hardened in anticipation.

The fire blazed, the tree sparkled, everyone smiled and sang, enjoying the moment. It filled him with overwhelming joy. This was his family. He looked at Gabby. His reaction was gut-wrenching. She fit in with his family better than he did. Perfect. The evening was perfect. Why had he stayed away so long?

Love—hard to contain, and even harder to fight.

When the last strains of *Silent Night* faded away, the last drop of hot chocolate sipped, and the last goodbyes given, Chad was ready to burst with joy at the headiness of it all. An audible sigh of relief slipped between his lips as the front door shut for the last time.

Finally. *Finally.* He and Gabby could be alone.

Chad turned back to the library. But it was empty.

Ethel appeared from the other direction, a tray in hand, prepared to pick up cups and crumbs from the impromptu family gathering.

"Here, Ethel, let me help you with those. As usual everything was great. What would this family do without you?"

"You're my family. And it's your family, too. Don't you forget it. You've stayed away much too long, and your mother misses you terribly. She wants to see you settled down, young man. Have babies of your own."

"Now, Ethel, don't you start. I've heard it all before. It's one of the things that keeps me away."

"It's not, and you know it. You stay away because you can't face facts. You want what everyone else has, but you're just too stubborn to admit it. You'll join the fray one day soon. Mind you, I think it's going to be sooner than anyone expects." Ethel smiled, and continued to collect the dirty dishes scattered around the room. "Here, take these to the kitchen while I gather the rest. Then take yourself off to bed. You look near to falling asleep on your feet after your long drive and full evening tonight."

Chad obeyed and carried the heavily laden tray to the kitchen. When he returned, he gave Ethel a quick hug and placed a quick kiss on her forehead. "You see too much. You know us too well. Which isn't always a good thing. People in my books die for less," he said with a grin.

"As long as you keep them in your books, young man. Now, go upstairs. You have a lot to think about."

She pushed him out the door toward the stairs. He let her.

She was right. He did have a lot to think about. In truth, he had already done a lot of thinking. What he needed now was to take action. He wasn't giving up. He was home for as long as it took to work things out with Gabby. That was a promise he'd already made to himself. Now, he just had to figure out his plan of action.

What would Dean Reynolds do? Dean was forceful, took control of every situation, and never let the girl call any of the shots. It was Dean's way or the highway. Maybe that's what he needed to be—forceful. Take her in his arms. Declare his love. And of course she would fall right into his arms and they would end up in bed, spending the night making mad, passionate love. *The End.*

God, just thinking about lying next to Gabby in bed had his BVDs stretching tight. He shut his eyes and pictured them together, naked, touching, kissing. His hands were touching her breasts. Now they were sliding down over her smooth, soft stomach and nearing…

A loud knock on his bedroom door startled him, bringing him out of his erotic daydream. He didn't even recall walking into his room or closing the door.

The knock sounded again. Chad shook himself, wiping the moisture from his forehead and upper lip. He needed a shave.

Chad took a deep, steadying breath before he opened the door. Gabby stood on the other side barefoot, wearing her bathrobe. Her magnificent auburn hair tumbled around her face. She made an enticing sight with her jade eyes wide, but cautious, yet all-knowing, as if they could look right through into his very soul. It was very disconcerting and at the same time very endearing. And seductive. Transfixed, Chad could only stare.

"What were you thinking?" Gabriella asked. "What makes you think you have to take care of Nina for the rest of her life?"

She stamped her foot and pointed those luscious fingers at his chest. If she touched him, he wasn't going to be responsible for his actions. He had worked himself into a lather over her mere moments ago. Spitfire or not, he wanted her now.

"Well, what have you got to say for yourself? I told you I didn't want your money. I'm not for sale. At any price."

Chad bit his tongue. There was always a price to pay—but he'd found out too late it didn't always have to be monetary. He hoped he wasn't too late. He was willing to pay any price—grovel if that's what it was going to take to make her listen to reason.

Her breasts rose and fell beneath her robe. He held

his breath. Was she naked beneath that tantalizing piece of material? She clutched the belt on her robe and drew it tighter. He let out the breath he'd been holding and reached for her.

"We need to talk, but I don't think now is the time. You're upset."

She skirted around him, her green eyes black with anger. Damn, she looked sexy. He wanted to kiss her rage away. Yes, she had every right to be mad at him for using Nina's trust fund as a means to help her, but it hadn't been out of sympathy—it had been out of love.

"Now is as good a time as any, so don't stand there and tell me to go away like a good little girl. I want answers, Chad, and I want them now. Why? Why did you go behind my back and make me think Tom had provided for her?"

"Simple. Because I knew you wouldn't accept my help any other way. I did it for Nina. I fell in love with the little tyke. I wanted to make sure she had security no matter what life brought her way."

"It's not simple at all and you know it. I told you we don't need your help."

"Listen, it's no big deal. I can afford it. I wanted to do it. It's done."

"I won't accept it."

"If you don't use it now, she gets whatever is left after her college expenses are paid, or when she turns twenty-five."

A defeated look came over her face. He wanted to wipe it away and make her smile again. She turned to walk out of his room. He pulled her back.

"I did it because I care—for you, too," he whispered. "I don't go around handing out money to everyone."

She hoped she wasn't making a mistake. Standing next to him in his room, so close, his hand on her arms, it was all she could do to stop from running into his arms. She'd been so angry at him once she'd figured out why Mindy and Dennis had been so evasive about signing papers for the trust fund, she'd kept her distance the rest of the evening. It had hurt, knowing he had devised a way to give her money. Lord, she had to admit it didn't stop her from wanting to be near him. His shirt hung open, exposing his broad chest and flat torso, and it was almost more than she could stand. She cleared her throat, the silence disconcerting.

His slate-blue eyes reminded her of a deep, turbulent ocean. His black hair tumbled over his forehead like a stalwart ship's captain standing at the helm on a stormy night at sea. She had the strongest urge to run her fingers through his hair. She started to lift her hand, caught herself and dropped it back to her side.

Chad caught the movement. She could see it in his mesmerizing eyes. She waited for his response, wished he would say something. Anything. But he didn't.

Caught in a world where nothing existed except the two of them, neither were capable of breaking the sexual tension spinning out of control around them. Gabriella couldn't move—didn't want to leave.

Chad finally broke the spell, his words softly spoken. "I've been a jackass, and I have no good excuse. God, Gabby, I'm sorry. Please forgive me for hurting you. And I'm sorry I didn't call you from New York or say goodbye before I left. The longer I left it, the harder it was to pick up the phone. I didn't want to talk about *us* over a damn phone," he growled.

Us? Her heartbeat raced. *Did he really believe there was an us? Especially after tonight?*

He rubbed his hands through his hair. "I wasn't sure of... well, you. *Us.* Where this whole thing was... is going."

"I understand. I know about the other women—Tanya—only wanting you for your money. It's not who I am. I don't need a lot of money to be happy." If she didn't leave soon, she wouldn't be able to leave at all.

He drew her further into his room—the contact magnetic. She sighed.

"I think it's great you care so much for Nina. But I feel as if I'm being bought off, damn you," she chastised him softly.

"Damn me all you want, just don't go. I've done nothing but dream about you all night. You've been driving me crazy with those come hither looks."

"Those were daggers I was throwing your way. I'm still upset."

"Then take your anger out on me. I deserve it. All of it."

Before Gabriella could respond, she found herself in Chad's arms. He covered her face with tentative kisses. By the time his lips met hers, her legs were about to give out—the kiss sapping the far reaches of her inner core. The overwhelming emotional tug on her heartstrings swept her away. She wrapped her arms around Chad and gave as good as she got—kiss for kiss.

His kisses became demanding, then became slow, sensual, and lingering. Her blood boiled and cascaded through her veins—intoxicating, heady. Drowning in a sea of emotional bliss, she didn't need or want to be rescued.

Chad slid his hands to the front of her robe and inched the soft fabric aside. The belt hung loose and fell away. The soft silky fabric of her nightshirt did nothing to impede the sensations his touch aroused. His fingers slid under the fabric, he cupped her bare breast in the palm of his hand. Gabriella's knees buckled. He caught her, swung her up into his arms, and closed the door with his foot.

"Steady, love," Chad said, nuzzling her neck. "I've waited all day to do this. Thank God, you're here now."

He kissed her tenderly, and whispered softly next to her trembling lips. He carried her to his bed, where he paused.

"Tell me to stop if you don't want this, Gabby. You've got to tell me, now."

"I want this," she breathed. "Don't stop now, Chad. Please."

"You've got to be sure, Gabby," he said, softly kissing her just below her earlobe, down her neck, across her bare shoulder, then lower.

Gabby shuddered—his lips and breath were feather light—erotic, mesmerizing. She held her own breath, but breathing wasn't necessary. The honesty in the moment was all-consuming—she allowed herself to be swept away.

"Yes," she whispered. "Oh, yes."

He laid her on the bed, and joined her.

A sense of longing so strong coursed through her. His ardent kisses were no longer enough. Gabriella clung to Chad like a lifeline—wanting, needing more. He pulled her into a crushing embrace that lasted a lifetime.

Coming up for air, Chad gently held her from him. She saw the truth of his need shining there for her to see. She wanted to tell him she loved him, right then and there. Wanted to shout it out loud to the world. But she held back, still afraid to share those words with another man. The assault on her senses continued as Chad rained more kisses on her lips, her neck, and finally the soft mound of her breast held firmly in his palm. Gabby didn't know when he had removed her robe, or her nightshirt, or his clothes, but she didn't care. He lifted her to heights far beyond her imagination.

Every part of his body touched every part of hers, and the heat of it had her in flames. She floated in midair, and the miracle of it all was that he seemed to be floating right along with her. Nothing in the whole world mattered right now except for his touch. Moonlight shone through the window as Chad softly stroked the length of her body. Several heated moments later, when they finally could wait no longer, Chad's fumbled attempt to enter her only to encounter a tender barrier Gabriella had guarded for so long.

He pulled back.

For a split second, Gabriella was afraid he would stop. She took matters into her own hands. Shy, but in the throes of passion, and in love with a man who she was afraid was about to leave her side, Gabriella placed her hands on Chad's firm, warm, hips and pulled him into her. In a heartbeat the discomfort forgotten, they found a rhythm that was theirs alone.

****

Chad lost it. Gabby was a virgin. It never occurred

to him that she hadn't had a physical relationship with Charles. The pounding of his heart matching hers was spiritual—their union ordained.

They lay together afterwards, his arms held her next to him. He was the luckiest guy in the universe. The gift she had just given him was a true blessing. A miracle.

Gabby snuggled closer, her head tucked comfortably under his chin. He smiled. He couldn't help it. He was her first lover—it was a heady and powerful sensation. On a more mundane level, he'd just bested Dean Reynolds, his fictitious love'em and leave'em heartbreaker hero in his novels. Maybe it was time for Dean to settle down and find his own special someone to spend the rest of his life with, too. Well, maybe not. Dean had a few more murder mysteries to solve before he retired. But Chad, although not ready to retire, was pretty sure he and Gabby could be happy together for a long time to come—if their spectacular lovemaking was any indication.

"Did I just wake up from a wonderful dream?"

"If it was a dream, I don't want to wake up," she murmured.

Chad pulled her into his arms and together they made love, slowly, passionately with both their hearts fully engaged. Again. And Again.

When he awoke the following morning, Chad was still smiling. He stretched, anticipating holding Gabby in his arms for an early morning nuzzle. But she wasn't there. He sighed. Then smiled again. She couldn't have gone far.

Chad jumped from bed, naked, grabbed his robe, and headed to the shower almost wishing Gabby would be there. But he was doomed to disappointment when there was no sign of her anywhere.

Half an hour later, refreshed from the warm pelting shower spray, Chad walked out a new man. Making love to Gabby had been like nothing he had ever experienced in his entire life. He couldn't wait to see her this morning, take her in his arms, and lavish kisses on her once again.

Dean Reynolds, eat your heart out!

Chapter Thirteen

"Oh, my God! What did I do last night?" Gabriella paced back and forth in her room. She'd never given herself to anyone before. But with Chad, it had felt so right—so wonderful. She'd missed him while he'd been in New York, and she'd fallen in love with the man. It must have been the wassail—she must have consumed too much of it during the caroling without realizing it. Of course, seeing him half naked in the moonlight in his bedroom had only heightened her own desires. But, Lord, to give herself to a man who hadn't even said he loved her? It was the most colossal mistake she'd ever made. How to explain her wanton behavior last night? In Chad's arms. In his bed. She cupped her hands to her face, the heat spiking just thinking about what she'd done. Oh, the passion of it, and now the regret.

No. She didn't regret having lain in his arms, having made love to him.

But, how was she ever going to face him this morning? And oh, what a field day Helen would have if she found out.

Gabriella procrastinated going downstairs.

Images of their lovemaking kept flashing in her mind. Her heart constricted, knowing Chad was not the marrying kind. He didn't need his orderly life spiraling out of control with a baby around all the time. Especially one who wasn't his. No matter what he said about caring for Nina, it wouldn't work. He needed uninterrupted time to write. She had to think of her future—hers and Nina's. Having an affair with Chad was not on her list, short or long-term, of goals and priorities. He was leaving for New York City right after Christmas. Only two more days left—she would make an effort to try to keep out of Chad's way. How hard could it be with him working in his room all day?

Memories of last night washed over her in great detail. She stomped her foot on the padded carpet as if it would chase all the sensual longings away. It didn't do a thing except bring tears to her eyes. He'd been so kind, caring and so very good at making love. No, facing him this morning wasn't going to be easy.

Gabriella forced her mind to focus on her responsibilities. She lifted Nina, freshly fed and changed and snuggled her in her arms. Nina squirmed, smiled, her eyes sparkling, and Gabriella's heart melted.

Gabriella entered the small morning room with Nina to find Chad drinking coffee and reading the morning paper. His elbow casually leaned on the table, his legs crossed. He looked vibrant, happy. Gabriella recalled just how securely and seductively those legs had been wrapped around her last night. She wanted to run for her life. Faltering, she turned to head in the opposite direction.

"Running away, Gabby?"

So much for escape. Resigned, she turned to face him. His magnetism after last night was powerful.

"Last night was a mistake. I had too much Wassail." She patted Nina's back, and rocked her back and forth.

"Really? Try again. It wasn't spiked—nothing but hot cider and orange juice. The cinnamon stick wasn't that potent." His dimpled smile stung.

"Don't make fun of me. I can't handle it right now." She spun away to avoid his probing eyes.

He stood, circled the table, and placed his hands on her shoulders. "It wasn't a mistake," he whispered.

He kissed her temple. She closed her eyes, allowing herself to savor his warm, affectionate touch. So much for keeping her distance.

"I'd never make fun of you." He placed another kiss to her cheek. "Please. Don't say it was a mistake."

She was afraid to look at him, his closeness driving her crazy. He smelled of fresh coffee, cinnamon, and uniquely Chad. He'd showered, but it hadn't washed away the tangy male scent of him from last night. Her face grew warmer just thinking about their lovemaking. His kiss infused her senses, and a flood of desire spiraled through her body. She shook herself free of the emotion, but it was useless. She would never be free of Chad. She would remember last night forever.

"We're good together, Gabby. Real good. You can't deny it." He continued to hold her while he ran a finger over Nina's chubby cheek.

Gabby's eyes focused on his finger, remembering how it had slid over her sensitized skin, and the things it made her feel.

"Chad, please…" She swallowed.

"You know I'm right. I told you..."

"Don't say it."

He put an arm around her, Nina now between them, and Gabby's legs almost gave out from the need his touch invoked.

"It's too soon. Last night was too soon." She couldn't meet his eyes.

"It's too right. Last night was too right. We're too right—the three of us are very right. I told you this munchkin has stolen my heart."

Gabriella leaned her head on his shoulder, a small moan escaping before she could call it back. She wanted to believe him.

"Tell you what," Chad whispered, "this afternoon when Nina's asleep, we'll talk. I want to spend time with you. Get to know the real you. For you to get to know the real me."

"Chad…"

"Gabby? What can it hurt? Just talk. I promise that's all it'll be. Although," his smile turned sexy, "I can't promise not to think about last night while we talk."

He kissed her temple. She had all to do to step back from the spell he was weaving around her like a dreamy sea mist. "It's not a good idea."

"Trust me, Gabby. Please," he whispered in her ear.

She looked up into his crystal blue eyes, now pleading with her to trust him. *How could she resist him when he looked at her like that?*

"Just talk," she whispered.

"Just talk," he confirmed. "Now sit. Have some breakfast. For some reason I'm ravenous this morning. How about you?"

His words, although meant to be playful, embarrassed her and made her on edge again.

"If that's the kind of talk you have in mind, I've changed my mind."

"What? What'd I say?" He threw his hands up in the air, and stepped back in a dramatic sweep of having done or said nothing wrong. "I'm hungry, that's all. Here, let me take Nina while you eat breakfast. Coffee's great. I've already had two cups."

Gabriella stared. Was she hearing right? Was he willing to hold Nina while she got something to eat? Sure, he'd said he cared for Nina, but to actually offer to hold her? She'd seen the look on his face the other day when he'd carried Nina over to Helen. Was this the same man who wanted nothing to do with kids? The same man who had guarded his well-ordered life for so long? Someone who'd sidestepped his mother's matchmaking like the plague because he didn't want to complicate his life? He wanted her to trust him? The man who trusted no one? Had he really changed?

Speechless, Gabby could only stand in disbelief as he took Nina from her and cuddled the small baby in his own arms.

"See—a piece of cake," he beamed.

When had he become so adept at holding a baby? And why did he look so natural and comfortable doing it?

"Are you sure…? You don't have to do this, you know. She's not your responsibility."

"Eat. I promise if she cries or spits up, she's all yours. In the meantime, Nina and I will sit here and get to know each other."

"You don't have to do this," she repeated. "I'm serious. Last night was a mistake."

"And I told you *I'm* serious. We'll talk later. We don't want to argue in front of the baby."

Gabriella sat. She liked the sound of that. It

sounded as if they were a married couple arguing. She could get used to being around this man day and night if she wasn't careful.

"This isn't going to work," she said. "Your life is perfect—uncluttered, successful. Mine is anything but."

He hadn't said he loved her—so where was this relationship going? She sipped her coffee, the warmth of it, usually soothing, did little to calm her shaky nerves.

"For the moment, but things will work out. We'll talk later. Now, eat," he ordered as if she were a stubborn child.

"Chad…"

"Do I have to take Nina in the other room so you'll eat? You need your strength. Eat. Pretend we aren't here."

"Like that's going to happen," she muttered in her coffee cup.

"I heard that."

She looked up. Oh, my. He was rocking Nina back and forth in his arms. But how long would his interest in Nina and her last? She had meant it when she said last night was a mistake. A wonderful mistake, but a mistake nevertheless. He hadn't said he loved her.

What exactly was he looking for in this relationship?

****

"Where are we going?" Gabriella asked, buttoning her jacket and wrapping her scarf around her neck later that afternoon. "It's too cold for a walk down by the lake."

Nina was snuggled warmly in her crib, the baby monitor on for Ethel in case the baby woke. Ethel had conveniently ignored them, not saying anything as Chad ushered her out the kitchen door. Embarrassed, Gabriella felt as if she was a teenager caught sneaking out on a clandestine date.

"Not where we're going. Come on, it isn't far." Chad put his hand on her back to get her started down the walk. He let his arms hang at his sides. "I have the perfect place where we can be alone without being disturbed. Trust me. You'll love it."

Trust him? She wanted to, she had to, she loved him.

The sun was high in the clear periwinkle sky, a slight breeze blew off the lake, and the snow-covered lawn was chilled. Chad stood next to her, not touching her, but still close enough she could breathe in his essence. His look was serious. She shivered, nervous at his intent. If he so much as touched her again, she'd turn and hightail it back to the house and safety. She'd been keyed up all afternoon just thinking about their "talk" and where their relationship was or wasn't going. She was afraid to find out.

She tucked her gloved hands in her pockets and tipped her head down against the wind. Chad didn't bother. He was enjoying the elements and the cool breeze coming off the lake. Thinking about their first kiss suddenly made her feel a little warmer, thinking about last night made her entire body explode like an overheated furnace.

The wind cooled her warmed cheeks as they circled the side lawn where snow-covered shrubs lined the cleared walkway. A full grove of Rhododendron, their leaves curled like tiny tubes to protect themselves from the cold, Azaleas tucked in between small evergreens, and Christmas Holly bushes sprinkled here and there lined the stairway leading down the slope to where the water met the shoreline. To the left stood an enchanting, enclosed white gazebo on a platform overlooking Cayuga Lake. In the summer it would be a great view of the many sailboats dotting the glistening waters. Now, the boats were tucked away for the winter. But the gazebo was glowing, the windowpanes frosted. Garlands circled the outside of the structure as if waiting for Santa to arrive. It looked inviting, cozy.

Too inviting. Too cozy.

Gabriella paused just as the wind picked up.

"Don't worry," Chad said behind her. "We'll be warm inside."

His words startled her. Had he read her mind, or had she spoken her thoughts aloud?

"I hope so. This wind is much colder next to the water."

Chad opened the glass door for her to enter. She stopped. He bumped into her.

Gabby looked around the closed interior. A small heater emitted warmth at the far end of the room. Scented candles flickered, casting a romantic atmosphere. Her heart melted. Cushions, piled high, lined the window seats, while others were scattered on the floor. A small table held a bottle of wine, and two fluted glasses waited to be filled.

"You set this up."

She turned on him, jabbed her finger into his firm chest, her first mistake—touching him.

"If you don't stop poking me with those sexy fingers of yours, I'm not going to be able to maintain control of my emotions. Obviously you don't know what they do to me."

"What are you trying to do? Seduce me? Again?"

"I want us to be comfortable. Relax."

"Relax? *Relax*? I know what you have in mind and I want no part of it. I told you…"

"Yeah, yeah, last night was a mistake. I know. I'm tired of hearing it. Especially when I know it was the most right thing I've ever done. You are the most right thing. You, Gabby. Only you."

He approached her.

She stepped back.

"Chad. Don't…"

He kissed her. Wrapped his arms around her. She lost what little fight was left in her and kissed him back. This was right where she wanted to be.

"See how perfect that was? How right we are together? Now that we've gotten that over with, let's sit down and talk."

Gabriella, in a daze over how easy he could melt her defenses, allowed Chad to lead her over to the window seat lined with pillows. She sat down. He unzipped her jacket and helped her out of it before taking his own jacket off. He sauntered over to the table and poured a wine that sparkled with the flickering of the candles. Mesmerized, she could no more take her eyes off him than she could stop breathing. His burgundy sweater and black slacks were a perfect match against his dark good looks. His black curls, windblown and hanging over his forehead made him look so boyishly handsome and so very enticing.

"Chad…"

"Here, drink this. Then we'll talk."

She sipped the wine, enjoying the tingle and

warmth as it slid down her dry, nervous throat. He settled next to her, close, and sipped from his own glass all the while watching her.

Close, very close, but not touching.

"God, Gabby, I want to wake up with you lying beside me every morning. After last night—the most incredible night of my life--I don't know how I can live without you by my side. You gave yourself to me... I'm speechless. I keep asking myself why? *Why me?*"

Gabriella opened her mouth. He smoothed a finger over her trembling lips.

"Don't tell me it was a mistake again. You have to let go of the past and trust me. I know I've let go. You can, too. I trust you with my heart."

Gabriella wanted to believe him.

"It's not that simple. I've Nina to think about now. She's my responsibility and I need to see this through on my own."

"We can do it together."

"For how long? How long until you tire of someone else's baby?"

"If she's part of your life, never."

She wanted a lifetime together with this man, but did he want a lifetime with her? Was he asking her to marry him? Hope blossomed in her heart.

"You also told me you didn't want me—need me."

Their eyes met.

"After last night, I know that's not true. Here, have more wine." He filled her glass.

"Nina and I are not a charity case."

Chad put his arm around her and held her close.

"I'm the charity case. I'm the one who's needy. Needy for you."

His nearness, his touch, his scent…dear, Lord…she wanted more. Much more. He leaned into her, their noses touched. The contact startled her. He inched her back into his arms and kissed her, leaving her in no doubt as to his need—leaving her trembling with a need of her own. Maybe it would work between them. Could she take the chance? She ended the kiss, but he wouldn't let her break from his hold. She found herself leaning into him, initiating a kiss of her own, and was lost. She threw her arms around his neck. Her glass tipped sideways—wine spilled to the floor.

"I love you, too," he whispered.

It took a moment for Gabby to realize what he'd said. She couldn't believe her ears.

"You love me? *Too*?"

"Yes."

"But I didn't say I love you."

"You trusted me enough last night to give yourself to me. It was the most precious gift anyone has ever given me."

"Oh, Chad," she whispered, still in his arms.

"Tell me it wasn't a mistake, Gabby. I need to hear you say it."

"It wasn't. It was so right. I was afraid you didn't love me as I love you."

"I think I've loved you and fought it since the first day we met," he said, lifting her fingers to his lips, kissing each fingertip in turn. "I've wanted to do this to these lovely fingers of yours since you jabbed them in my chest when I bumped into your car."

The sensation sent erotic waves through her overheated body. What this man could do with his tongue was driving her wild. Gabby threw herself back into his willing arms, and together they slipped to the floor. Chad gathered more pillows as they went. He grabbed the afghan at the last minute.

As the afternoon sun descended over the hilltops, Gabriella nestled in Chad's arms—a lethargic, sensual cocoon enveloped them. Candles flickered against the windowpanes and as Gabriella lay on the floor next to Chad, she looked up to find one of the biggest kissing balls she'd ever seen.

"Chad?"

"Hmmm."

"Did you hang the mistletoe up there this afternoon?"

"Hmmm."

"Why?"

He stirred and rolled her around to face him. "I wanted you to have good memories under a mistletoe, not the mistakes of the past."

She kissed him and nuzzled into his chest, her hand leisurely rubbing her fingers over his tight abs.

"Thank you," she choked.

He chuckled. "Did it work?"

"Oh, yes. You know it did."

Gabby smiled, happy to be in his arms again. Right where she wanted to be—forever.

"Come with me to New York," Chad whispered. "We can fix up a room for Nina until we decide where we want to live. The city is no place for a baby. Do you like horses? I was thinking maybe we need to find somewhere in the country. Someplace where we can raise horses."

"Horses?"

"Hmmm. My grandfather used to have a horse

farm out in the country. I loved it."

Gabriella let him ramble, enjoying the pictures in her mind of a large house, kids playing in the yard, a horse ranch—a family of her own. With her own family gone, just thinking about one with Chad was like an answer from the gods above. Yes. She'd love to have a family with him. But she wanted to finish her degree first, and hoped he'd understand.

"I can't go to New York. I need to stay here and finish my Master's degree. I only have one semester to complete."

"I don't know if I can be away from you that long now I've found you," he said, sitting and settling her spoon-fashion between his outstretched legs. He wrapped the afghan around her, tucking it snugly up under her arms. He kissed her head as it lay nestled under his chin, heady, protected, safe, warm, and thoroughly loved.

"I know. I don't want to be away from you, either. But I do want to finish my degree and get everything squared away with Nina."

Chad placed his hands on her shoulders and gently squeezed them. "We'll find a way."

When the sun set in the winter sky, with the wind whipping at their backs, they made their way back to the house. White flakes swirled down around them. Gabriella snuggled into Chad's arms, but her spirits had dropped along with the outside temperature—Chad hadn't said a word about marriage.

****

Helen and Ethel beamed when Chad joined them in the library for drinks before dinner. The Christmas parties were over.

"So, Junior, I see you and Gabriella have patched up your differences. How nice. About time, too. Why, I'm so pleased I found her for you. She's just what you need."

"Mother, you didn't find her for me. She fell in your lap and you were given the opportunity of a lifetime. Admit it, you had nothing to do with it at all."

His mother smiled mysteriously, but nodded. "If you say so, dear. If you say so. Ethel, why don't you go see what's keeping our Gabriella while I have a talk with my son."

"Don't be too hard on him, Helen. He'll do the right thing. Just you give the boy a chance."

"No doubt he'll do the right thing. After all, he's a Hempstead and the Hempsteads always do the right thing."

"Stop talking about me as if I'm not here. Of course I plan to do the right thing. I love the girl, for crying out loud. Why wouldn't I?"

Ethel grinned on the way out of the room. His father entered seconds later.

"What right thing are you talking about, Son?" Chad's father asked. He held the door for Ethel, moved to his wife's side and gave her a kiss on the cheek. "You look very festive this evening, my dear. Am I missing something? What's our son been up to now?"

"Nothing. Can we change the subject?" Chad took a deep breath. His parents were exasperating. He didn't want to share his feelings for Gabriella with them quite so soon.

"Why, Chad just told me he and Gabriella are in love. Isn't that wonderful, dear?"

"It's about time he acknowledged it," his father

said, smugly.

Chad wasn't about to encourage the two of them any further. But during dinner, his mother couldn't keep her excitement to herself.

"My dear. It's such wonderful news about you and Chad. Love is so romantic this time of year, don't you agree?"

Gabriella choked on her chicken. *Helen thought there was going to be a wedding. Was there going to be a wedding?* She looked at Chad over the rim of her glass, wondering just what he had told his parents.

Chad shrugged his shoulders. Helen kept right on talking.

"Now, I know your sisters are going to be so excited when I tell them the news. They've seen this coming, too. Right, Chadwick?" Helen turned to her beaming husband.

There was no need for anyone to respond. Helen wasn't looking for an answer—she had it all figured out.

Finally, Chad interrupted his mother. "If you'll excuse us, I think this is the part where Gabby and I want to be alone."

Taking Gabby's hand, he led her out of the room and up the stairs out of earshot.

"You look done in. Why don't you have an early night."

He kissed her, deeply, thoroughly, and sensually. He opened her bedroom door.

"I'll see you in the morning."

Gabby was disconcerted and confused by his simple goodnight kiss before he turned and walked to his own room.

Chapter Fourteen

Everyone attended Midnight Mass, including Helen, who had rested most of the day so she could handle the strain of getting to and from the house to the car, to the church, and back again. During the candlelight service, Chad sat next to Gabby, his presence a comfort. Gabby held Nina in her lap, and reflected on her sister and brother-in-law, her parents, and the family that would never get to celebrate a holiday with Nina, or see her grow to be a young woman. She sent up a silent prayer for them, and one for herself that she would be able to do right by her niece.

Chad wrapped his arm around her, as if he read her mind. She leaned her head on his shoulder and accepted the reassurance he provided. His strength gave her the courage to be strong.

When they returned home after the candlelight service, Nina had fallen asleep. Gabriella tucked her in bed for the night, making sure the baby monitor was turned on before joining the others downstairs. A fire blazed in the grate while soft Christmas music played in the background. The entire family, including all the children, were gathered around the tree.

"Come. Join us for a Christmas toast," Helen said.

"We get to open presents tonight," Constance said. "I want to open this one first."

"Only one present tonight," Helen reminded her grandchildren.

Chadwick began handing out gifts from under the tree to his grandkids.

"Tomorrow we open Santa's presents, but tonight we share ours with each other."

Chad sat beside Gabriella on the couch, and handed her a small box.

"For you," he said. "I couldn't resist."

The package was too large for a ring box. She chided herself for being so indulgent with her dreams. Of course he wasn't giving her a ring. She put on a brave face and took her time opening the present. Once opened, she couldn't contain her laughter.

"My slipper socks. Where did you find them? I've been looking all over for them," she said. "Oh." She remembered when Chad first kissed her under the mistletoe.

A devilish grin spread across his face. Embarrassed, she looked around the room only to find everyone ignoring them as they busily opened their own presents.

"Here, this goes along with it," he said, handing her another box, bigger this time.

Gabriella hid her disappointment again. She took the larger box from Chad and opened it. Inside was another wrapped package. Curious, Gabriella lifted the smaller box out and tore the brightly colored paper off it only to discover yet another smaller container. This one was an unwrapped velvet jeweler's box. The smaller box was locked, but there was no key to be found.

"I think this is what you're looking for," Chad said,

handing her a small gold key. "The key to my heart. Go ahead. Open it."

Gabriella's hands shook, making it hard to insert the key in order to turn the lock. Once opened, she stared at the glistening diamond nestled in the jeweler's box. Stunned at the significance of it and his words, she looked from the ring to Chad, then back down at the ring.

"Oh, Chad. It's beautiful. I was so afraid you…that is…you only…"

"Will you marry me, Gabby?"

She looked into his eyes and was overjoyed at the love shining there.

"How can I say no with your entire family waiting with bated breath? Yes. Oh, yes, Chad. I'd love to marry you."

Chad kissed her in front of the family while they all clapped and cheered in unison.

"Uncork the champagne so we can celebrate," Chad's father said to no one in particular.

"I didn't say a word. Honest. No one here knew I was going to ask you to marry me tonight. I swear."

Chad's father passed around the champagne for the adults and sparkling grape juice for the children. Everyone raised their glasses and toasted the newly engaged couple.

Chad kissed her again, sipped from his glass, all the while drinking in her happiness before whispering in her ear. "I love you, Gabby. I don't want a long engagement. Let's plan a New Year's Day wedding. We'll live here until you finish your master's degree, then we'll take an extended honeymoon while we wait for Nina's adoption papers to be finalized. What do you think, love?"

"I love you," Gabriella sighed. "It sounds wonderful. New Year's Day can't come soon enough."

This time Gabby kissed Chad. The entire family sent up another round of cheers as Chad slipped the ring on her finger.

A word about the author...

Carol Henry is an author of Destination: Romance—Exotic Romantic Suspense Adventures (*Amazon Connection*; *Shanghai Connection*), as well as contemporary romance and historic women's fiction. She is an international traveler and travel writer of exotic locations for major cruise lines' deluxe in-cabin books.

Carol lives with her husband in the beautiful New York State Finger Lakes region where they are surrounded by family and friends. The holidays are special occasions at the Henry household, especially Christmas—so it's no surprise that *Nothing Short of a Miracle* is full of many memorable family gatherings and events.

You may visit Carol's website at:
http://www.carolhenry.org.